JUMPSTART THE WORLD

JUMPSTART THE WORLD
Catherine Ryan Hyde

Alfred A. Knopf

New York

THIS IS A BORZOI BOOK PUBLISHED BY ALFRED A. KNOPF

Visit us on the Web! www.randomhouse.com/teens

Educators and librarians, for a variety of teaching tools, visit us at
www.randomhouse.com/teachers

Library of Congress Cataloging-in-Publication Data
Hyde, Catherine Ryan.
Jumpstart the world / Catherine Ryan Hyde. — 1st ed.
p. cm.
Summary: Sixteen-year-old Elle falls in love with Frank, the neighbor who helps her adjust
to being on her own in a big city, but learning that he is transgendered turns her world
upside down.
ISBN 978-0-375-86665-4 (trade) — ISBN 978-0-375-96665-1 (lib. bdg.) —
ISBN 978-0-375-89677-4 (ebook)
[1. Moving, Household—Fiction. 2. High schools—Fiction. 3. Schools—Fiction.
4. Transgendered people—Fiction. 5. Apartment houses—Fiction. 6. Mothers and daughters—
Fiction.] I. Title.
PZ7.H96759Jum 2010
[Fic]—dc22
2010002511

The text of this book is set in 11-point Goudy.

Printed in the United States of America
October 2010
10 9 8 7 6 5 4 3 2 1

First Edition

For my good friend Douglas.
May you live a long and
healthy life.

ONE

How My Weird Cat Got His Weird Name

"This is a *beautiful* cat," my mother said. She was staring into a cage at about eye level.

I sidled over just enough to get a peek at the cat in question. A long-haired silvery Persian mix. He was beautiful all right, in an aloof sort of way. I'm not a big fan of aloof. Besides, I already had a cat in mind. I just hadn't found the nerve to announce it yet.

Here's the first thing I need to tell you about my mother: she uses the words "beautiful" and "ugly" a lot. And I do mean a lot. I think she does it unconsciously. I try to tell her how much she does it, but she says I'm exaggerating. Sometimes I feel like I want to make a secret tape of one of her monologues about the world. I could count the number of times she used those two words. I could prove it to her.

Lately I've been noticing how people have these ways of accidentally letting you see what's important to them.

I know it doesn't sound like any big deal. But it is to me. Because I'm not beautiful. And we both know it. Anyone with eyes knows it.

My mother and I were at the Department of Animal Services shelter, choosing a new cat to keep me company in my new place. I'd lost custody of our cat, Francis, in the move. No matter how much I argued matters of fairness, Francis would stay with my mother. Why I thought I would win that point, I'm not sure. I never won any others.

She'd tried to talk me into a cat from our fancy, expensive midtown pet store. The pound was my idea. I think it's indecent and inhumane to spend hundreds of dollars on a pedigreed cat while all these sweet, deserving animals are dying because nobody wants them. It's just so unfair.

Finally. A point I could win.

"I want *this* one," I said.

My mother had a way of moving across a room. I'm not sure how to describe it. Except . . . you know the way an actress floats onto the stage to accept an Academy Award? Like that. She was wearing shiny black tights and her short red leather jacket. There were multiple things wrong with this picture. The first was a leather jacket on an eighty-degree day. Then there was the issue of the tights. Only nineteen-year-olds should wear black tights with nothing on over them. No, I take that back. Nobody should.

I guess she figured she could pull it off because she'd had a lot of plastic surgery. Probably even *I* didn't know the whole of it. She'd begun lying to everyone, taking what she called "spa vacations" and coming back with fewer wrinkles and a smaller butt.

I held my ground and continued to point into the cage that held my new cat. He was huddled in the back corner, like he was trying to disappear. At the front of the same cage was an ordinary-looking orange tabby blinking at me.

"Okay, now please tell me why that one. That cat is so . . . There is nothing distinctive or beautiful about that cat. I wish you would look at this beautiful Persian mix again. Why you would settle for that plain-looking tabby . . ."

"Not that one," I said. "The black one. The guy in the back."

In the silence that followed, it was all I could do to keep from smiling. This was the cat that would drive my mother crazy. This was the choice only I could make.

First of all, he had only one eye. The other was just closed forever, like nothing had ever been there. And he had a big chunk bitten out of his right ear, and patches of missing fur. He looked like his hair had been falling out in clumps.

He was perfect. He was my cat.

Long, long silence.

"Okay," she said. Quietly. Then, measuring every word: "You're angry with me. I understand that. I'm not even saying I blame you—"

"I'm taking that cat. I want the black one. You can't talk me out of it, so don't even try." I was already starting to understand him. To feel for him. Or maybe even to feel *with* him. He was scared. He was not cuddly. He was not beautiful. If I didn't take him, he was as good as dead. He was about to be given the death penalty for not being beautiful. Someone had to come along and love him just the way he was. I was that someone. "It's not about being angry with you. Everything isn't always about you, Mother."

But, truthfully, somewhere in the back of my mind I think I knew it was both. Probably so did she.

*   *   *

This next thing that happened is important. It was one of those moments. I'm fascinated by moments like this. Always have been. The kind where you think something really ordinary is happening, so ordinary that you're barely even paying attention. But then, looking back, you see it wasn't ordinary at all. It was maybe the most important thing that ever happened to you. But at the moment you lived it out, it barely even blipped onto your radar screen.

I go back a lot and think about the time I first met Frank. It's sort of mind-boggling, to compare how important it turned out to be with how important I thought it was at the time. But I guess it doesn't help to go on and on about weird stuff like that.

Anyway, we were walking down the hall. My mother and me. Walking down my new hall, toward the door of my new apartment. I was lugging the cat carrier, which was getting pretty heavy. I kept thinking my mother would offer to take it from me for just a minute. Give me a chance to breathe. But maybe she was still mad that I didn't take the beautiful Persian. Either that or she was afraid ugliness might be contagious.

The door of the apartment next to mine opened, and there was Frank. Only, I didn't know it was Frank at the time, like I was saying before. He was just this little guy, standing out in the hall. He was probably even an inch or two shorter than me. But then I'm pretty tall—about five nine. I figured him to be maybe thirty or so. He had dark hair that was cut really short, short enough that it stuck straight up on top, and little round wire-rimmed glasses. Pretty thick glasses, too. There was something kind of elfin about him. At least, I remember thinking that at the time. Now I look back and can't imagine seeing him as anything but brave and big. But at the time, I remember getting images of pixies and leprechauns.

"Moving in!" he said. "Welcome." He had a funny voice, like he'd been sucking helium. Well, not that funny. I'm exaggerating. But it definitely reinforced the elflike image. He made "welcome" sound like the short version of "Welcome to Munchkin Land." And as far as the "moving in" comment goes, I tend to have issues with people who restate the obvious. At least, when my mother does that, it drives me crazy. But it was hard to fault a guy like Frank, and I don't just mean in hindsight. I mean even at the time. He had a big, friendly smile, and there was something cute about him, but in a soft sort of way. Hard to explain what I mean by soft. Gentle, I guess I mean. He made you try not to find fault with him for some reason. The kind of guy it's hard not to like.

"Need any help? I'm small, but I'm strong." He flexed a bicep, pulling up his T-shirt sleeve. Not the biggest muscles in the world, I guess, but definitely muscles. And besides, it was sort of funny and nice, the way he did that.

"Thank you, young man," my mother said, totally humiliating me. I mean, who calls someone young man, anyway? It's so demeaning. And besides, he was only about ten years younger than she was. I felt my face flush red. "But we've hired moving men. The boxes have already arrived."

"Well, if there's anything I can do for my new neighbors . . ."

My mother just continued to sweep down the hall to my new apartment door. In that weirdly dramatic way she has of doing things.

I stood in front of my new door with this heavy cat, waiting for my mother—who had the key—to actually let us in. But she threw me a curve, hanging a sudden U-turn and sweeping back down the hall to New Neighbor Guy. I set down the cat carrier and sighed.

"There is *one* thing you could do for me. My daughter will be on her own for the very first time. And in this big, ugly city, too." There it was again. Ugly. I had begun counting. "And she's so young. Turned eighteen barely a minute ago." She cut her eyes back to me. We had a quick little argument, just with our eyes and our faces. With my eyes and face I said, You're a liar and I can call you on it anytime. And with her eyes and face she said, This is for your own good, hush, and then my eyes and face said I didn't believe a word of what her eyes and face had just said. Mother and I fought so well we didn't even need to talk anymore. Fighting with actual words was optional. "Maybe I could leave you with an emergency number. Just in case. I *do* worry about her."

"I can use a phone, Mother."

"Not if you're hurt or in trouble you can't. Let me give the nice young man my number."

I rolled my eyes and waited. I was thinking, If you were really afraid of me getting hurt or in trouble, you'd let me live at home. Like other fifteen-year-olds do.

The minute I opened the carrier, the cat hissed at me. Then he leaped straight up in the air, landed on the hardwood floor, and ran under the bed.

My mother was busy trying to pretend he didn't exist.

"Now, Donald is taking me to dinner at Café del Arte. But the minute I'm done eating, I'll be over to help you unpack. I should be back by eleven."

"I'll be in bed by eleven."

"You can stay up just this one night."

"I have my first day of school in the morning. You know. New school? New year? Kind of a big deal?"

"One night. You're young. It won't kill you. When I was your age, I burned the candle at both ends, and I'm still here."

It takes me a long time, usually, to get mad. I'm not one of those people who flies off the handle easily. I have a pretty long fuse. But I felt myself rise up to something, and I knew it was not about to be contained. Frankly, I suspect it had been a long time coming. A long, painful buildup.

"How many different ways do I have to tell you that I'm not you," I said, without raising my voice, "before you actually get it?" She stared at me, quite silent. I'm sorry to have to admit that it was gratifying. But I wasn't done. Not nearly. "I really wish you would stop pretending this is fun. And that we're doing it together. If you tell me one more time that it's just like having a wonderful new room, I'm going to scream. A wonderful new room wouldn't be across town from the other rooms in our apartment—"

She unwisely attempted to interject: "Now, you know how hard I looked for something closer—"

"Just listen," I said. "For once in your life, just listen."

That surprised even me. It surprised her even more. It took her a while to close her mouth. But she said nothing.

"This is not fun," I said. "It sucks. I hate it. If you're going to do it, fine. Do it. And if you want to pretend it's a wonderful adventure, I guess there's not much I can do to stop you. But I won't pretend with you. I choose not to pretend. Now go have dinner with Donald. I'll unpack my own things."

Silence. Not the most fun silence ever. A wounded sort of a silence. Like we were watching some living thing lying on the floor bleeding.

"Someday you'll understand," she said. After a truly painful length of time.

"I doubt it."

"You'll fall in love someday yourself."

"Not like that, I won't."

Another difficult pause.

"I'm sorry, Elle," she said.

"Right. Whatever."

She let herself out. Slammed the door a little harder than necessary.

I looked at the stack of unpacked boxes, sitting like Mt. Elle in my new living room. I slammed into the tower and sent it all tumbling. I heard my new cat skitter, undoubtedly from one hiding place to another. I could hear his claws scrambling over the wood floor. I slapped the coffeemaker Mother had given me and sent it flying onto the kitchen linoleum, where the carafe shattered. I didn't drink coffee. She drank coffee. If she could see where she left off and I began, she'd know that.

I looked around for something else to break, but everything else was packed. If I wanted to break something else, I'd have to find it first, and that really dampened the mood and the moment.

I sat on the floor for a few minutes with my head in my hands.

Somebody knocked on the door. I pretty much assumed it was my mother, coming back. I think, in a weird way, I wanted it to be. I think I never entirely believed she'd go through with this thing. Part of me kept expecting to suddenly find out it wasn't going to happen like this for real.

"Who is it?"

"Your neighbor, Frank Killborn. From next door?"

Oh. Right. Munchkin Guy.

8

I got up and answered the door. I didn't open it very wide. "Sorry about the noise," I said.

"It's not that. Just wanted to be sure you were okay. Sounded like somebody was killing somebody over here."

"Well, they must have been killing somebody else," I said. "Because I'm fine."

"Good," Frank said. "Now I don't have to call your mother."

We both smiled a little. It was awkward. You get to a point where you either have to stop talking or open the door wider.

"I'd ask you in, but I'm not unpacked at all. . . ."

"No problem. Not trying to intrude. Just—"

Out of the corner of my eye, I saw a black flash. He streaked by me along the floor and out into the hall. I tried to reach down and grab him, but it was too late. "Oh shit. My cat!"

"I'll get him," Frank said.

"Don't. He'll kill you. He's not friendly at all."

We ran down the hall after him. Frank managed to get between the cat and the stairs, which was good because pretty soon after that, the cat ran out of hall. Frank cornered him and closed in.

"He'll scratch you," I said.

"I'm a vet tech. I know how to handle a scared cat."

He reached down and held the cat by the scruff of his neck, gently pinning him to the hall carpet. Then, with his free hand, he scooped up the cat and got him pinned to his side without so much as a fight.

"There's a trick," he said. "You hold them like this. Their front legs in your hand like so. Then pin their back legs against your hip with your elbow. That way they can't scratch with either their front or back claws. And as long as you have the scruff of their neck, they can't bite."

9

"There's an even better trick," I said. "Get a friendly cat."

We brought him back inside and I closed the door, quickly. Closed me and the cat and the neighbor into my apartment.

Then I felt weird because I was in there with this guy I didn't know. But I never actually thought he'd hurt me or anything. You couldn't think that with Frank. It just didn't fit.

He put the cat down. I suppose it goes without saying that the cat immediately ran and hid.

"Thanks," I said.

"No problem."

We just stood there for a minute in that sea of tumbled boxes. I was hoping he'd go home.

I said, "I'm beginning to think I made a mistake, getting that cat. I was trying to piss my mother off. But now she's gone, and it doesn't bother her, and I have to live with him. And he's supposed to be all I have to keep me company in this new place. I'm beginning to wish I'd gotten something more cuddly. You know, a cat I could actually hug. I don't know what I was thinking. It was stupid."

Speaking of stupid, what was I telling him all this for? It was so unlike me, to actually talk to somebody like that. And I didn't even know Frank.

"Maybe this guy'll come around."

"Maybe." Probably right around the time I got used to living alone.

A really awkward moment, and then he said, "Well, okay, then."

And I said, "Thanks for coming by."

And he said, "If there's anything we can do to help you settle in . . ."

I didn't know who or what constituted the rest of that "we," but I wasn't dying to open up any new subjects. I just wanted to get past this "new neighbor" part of things and be alone again.

"Thanks," I said. "Thanks for coming by."

He let himself out. And then, the minute he did, I didn't want to be alone anymore. And couldn't imagine why I'd ever thought I did.

I looked around for my cat. I found him right where I expected to find him—hiding under the bed. It suddenly hit me that I'd better unpack the litter box and litter, preferably right away.

Lots of things were beginning to dawn on me. Like the fact that if I wanted to take a shower, I actually had to find soap and shampoo. And towels and washcloths. And hang the shower curtain. Like the fact that there was zero food in the fridge. Like the fact that I actually *lived* in this strange new place. And that nothing was set up for me the way it had been at home.

It took me almost twenty minutes to find the bag from the pet store, with the cat food and litter box and the bag of kitty litter. Among all those spilled mountains of bags and boxes. I set it up in the corner of the bathroom. Filled it with litter. There was a slotted plastic scoop in the bag. Probably for cleaning out the box.

That's when it hit me. A whole new level of dawning. There would be no maid to clean out the litter box. Not now, not ever. I was the maid now.

I went back to the bedroom and got down on my hands and knees. Looked in at the cat. I could see his one gold eye glowing in the dark. He hissed at me.

I said, "Toto, I don't think we're in Kansas anymore."

And that is how my weird cat got his weird name.

TWO

Isn't Annie Lennox Straight?

I woke up weirdly early. That time of day you know in your gut is the middle of the night, but that the clock insists on labeling "morning." Though it would certainly be fair to qualify it as the wee hours.

I decided to plug in my computer, and at least get it set up. See if I could single-handedly get it to work with the Internet connection I had just inherited.

I found about fifteen pieces of spam mail, and a note from my mother.

The subject line said "Exciting News."

My heart fell. Don't ask me why. It's something about how well I know my mother. When she says a thing like that, she means it's exciting for *her*. And I'm not going to like it.

I know that sounds like too much to gather from a two-word subject line.

Except I was right.

The e-mail said the following: "Donald's taking me on a cruise. It was a surprise! Isn't that just the best? We leave Monday." My stomach dropped again. Farther this time. The day before my birthday. Donald was whisking her off on a cruise the day before my birthday. "But don't worry. When I get back, we'll throw the best party ever. Just slightly belated. After all, what's in a date? Love, Mother."

What's in a date? Oh, I don't know. Like . . . a birth?

I felt myself grinding my molars together too hard.

I looked around. It was still dark in my weirdly empty apartment. I could see a little bit of my surroundings by the glow of the streetlight outside. The shadow of the fire-escape railing against the window. Boxes on the bare hardwood floor. There was something spooky about the starkness and the shadows. Something I couldn't seem to shake.

I felt cheated because I'd already used up my best temper tantrum. All the boxes were spilled across the floor where I couldn't even smash into them in my rage. Anything I did after that would seem anticlimactic.

I looked under the bed, but no cat. Looked in the closet. Nothing. I walked around the place a little, turning on lights.

I finally found him in the bathroom, huddled in the tub. I couldn't even see him until I pulled back the shower curtain, which I had gone to great trouble to hang before bed.

When he saw me, he lifted straight up into the air and then scrambled to take off. I could hear the awful noise of his claws on the porcelain. The scene seemed to play out in slow motion, because he couldn't get any traction. I felt like I was watching a character in a cartoon, that weird exaggeration of a simple motion. It almost made me laugh. But underneath the humor of the situation was that other side of the thing—the part that wasn't funny in any way.

When he finally managed to launch out of the tub, he accidentally ran across my foot, drawing blood with a couple of his back claws.

After about ten minutes of looking for Band-Aids in a few miscellaneous boxes, I gave up and wrapped my foot in toilet paper.

I generally try not to waste a lot of time feeling sorry for myself. Some days are harder than others.

Later that morning, when the hours slowly grew less wee, I found an entirely new way to release my anger. And it wasn't anticlimactic at all. In fact, it was original, creative, and altogether satisfying.

I cut off all my hair.

Mother loved my hair. So of course she would be horrified. Which hardly prevented my decision to do the thing. If anything, it may have been part of the incentive.

Of course, she loved my hair because it was so much like her hair. We're both natural redheads. Or, at least, we both started out that way. Now she dyes hers red to cover God-only-knows-how-much gray. But, natural or not, we both have lots of red hair, thick and long and a little bit wavy.

I'd run down to the Duane Reade to get Band-Aids, and while I was there I'd made an impulse purchase. I got one of those clippers men use to keep their beards neat. You can set it to different lengths. I set it as long as it goes, so I wouldn't literally be bald. All that thick red hair dropped onto the bathroom tiles, just like that.

It came out a little bit longer than Frank's. But it was still short enough to stick up on top.

I liked it. I thought it made me look like a model. It made me look radical and dangerous and a little scary.

I looked at myself in the mirror for a long time. I thought I looked like Annie Lennox, back when she was half of the Eurythmics. Or a young Annie Lennox, anyway. Or maybe like a young Annie Lennox would look without all that makeup.

Looking back, I think if I made a list of all the things I've done that were . . . well, I don't want to say stupid. I don't want to be self-abusive here. A list of things that might have warranted rethinking—how does that sound? I think going to my first day of the new school year at a new school with a more or less shaved head, well . . . that might have found a good home on the aforementioned list.

Don't get me started on *why* it's a new school. Let's just say all disastrous changes track back to The Donald, who found my current high school "pricey" and "coddling."

But I'll just get too upset if I talk about it, so that's another rant for another day.

Anyway, it was probably lousy thinking, but I guess I wasn't really thinking. I was in more of a feeling mode. And what I was feeling was pissed.

The morning passed for normal. Nobody really seemed to pay attention to my head. Except me. I was weirdly aware of it all morning. Like I could feel people looking at it. But most of the time, they weren't. I mean, as far as I could see. I was the invisible girl. They weren't looking at any part of me at all.

So I thought.

Then, coming back from lunch, I saw somebody's locker had gotten graffitied. Some idiot had taken a spray-paint can with a narrow tip—the kind kids use for tagging—and painted the word "QUEER" on somebody's locker. They'd painted it vertically, with the Q on the top, and it covered the whole locker.

How humiliating. For somebody.

When I got close enough to read the locker numbers, turned out the somebody was me.

I kept double-checking the number. Thinking I was making a mistake. I had to be. I mean, new school—I just forgot the number. But it checked against the number I'd written on the inside cover of my notebook. Still, it wasn't until my key fit the lock that it hit me. The insult really had been meant especially for me.

I looked around to see a group of older boys watching me. Waiting to see what I would do. They looked pretty pleased with themselves.

"I'm not gay," I said.

They laughed and walked off down the hall.

I'm not gay. Why would somebody paint that on my locker? I'm not gay. Must have been a case of mistaken identity.

Or the haircut.

I thought it made me look like Annie Lennox. I didn't think it made me look gay.

I had no idea what to do about the locker, so I just walked away.

I went into the girls' room and looked at myself in the mirror, trying to see if I looked more Annie Lennox or more gay. I guess it sort of depended on how you looked at me. When I looked for Annie, I saw her, but when I looked for gay, I guess I saw something that might have given somebody the wrong idea.

Then all of a sudden, there was this girl standing right behind me. I saw her in the mirror, and spun around. She was short, and heavy, with hair not much longer than mine, only it was dyed blue. She was wearing a top that didn't cover her whole midriff. She had a ring in her nose.

She looked gay. Actually.

"Here," she said. She handed me a cleaning rag made from half an old towel, and a metal can of paint thinner.

Probably I should have said thanks, but it just happened so fast. "You just walk around carrying paint thinner?"

"We've all been there," she said. I guess she meant the locker. I figured, yeah, she probably had. She looked like she would have to take that kind of crap on a pretty regular basis.

"How do I get this back to you?"

"I'll be right here," she said. "I'm not going to French today. I'll be in here having a smoke or two all period. When you get the locker cleaned up, you can bring it back."

She lit a cigarette.

I went off to clean my locker, and it wasn't until I was most of the way down the hall that I realized I never did say thank you.

When I got back to the girls' room, she was still there. Still smoking.

"Thanks," I said. "That really saved my ass."

"No worries."

I went over to the sink and washed out the towel as best I could, and washed my hands. My hands still smelled a little like paint thinner, even after I scrubbed them raw.

She just stood there, half in an open stall, smoking and watching me. Then she said, "You can hang with us if you want."

17

"I'm not gay," I said. Sounding a little ticky, I think. "I don't know why people are saying this stuff about me. I just cut my hair to piss off my mother."

"I didn't ask if you were gay. I just said you could hang with us."

"Oh," I said. And then felt really embarrassed. "You meant either way."

"Yeah."

"So you were actually just being nice."

"Pretty much."

"So I was being . . . like . . . a total jerk."

"Pretty much."

"Sorry."

"Whatever."

"No, really. I mean, seriously. I'm sorry for being a jerk to you. I actually try really hard not to be. I try to spend as little time as possible being a jerk. But then sometimes I find out I just was. Already. And it's too late. You know?"

"Special dispensation," she said. "You're having a bad day."

"Thanks," I said. "I'll take it."

It was a hot afternoon, but I didn't know it for real until I got out of the air-conditioned school. I walked home instead of taking the subway. I turned on the air conditioner in my apartment for just a few minutes.

I hate air conditioners. In our old apartment, Mother always kept the place like a deep freeze. She had this thing about sweating. She never wanted it to happen to her. She viewed sweating as something that happened to lower-class strangers only. The air in that place always felt so unnatural.

After a while, I turned it off and opened all the windows. Then I crawled out onto the fire escape and sat outside my window, just watching the city go by underneath.

I watched cabs bunch up and then go again, heard them honk their horns. I watched people bustle by down there, and heard the sirens of fire trucks or ambulances I never saw. Sometimes I could smell the cigarette smoke all the way up on the third floor. The exhaust smell was constant. You almost forgot you were breathing fumes after a while.

The air never really moved out there. It felt thick and heavy, like there was barely enough to breathe.

I heard Frank's voice say, "Radical new haircut."

I looked over and saw he was on the fire escape outside his window. I don't know how long he'd been there.

"Yeah," I said. "Another bright move. Just about as smart as the cat."

Speaking of the cat, I hadn't seen him since I got home. I'd have to be careful he didn't scoot out the open window.

"Sorry you did it now?"

"Yeah. Kind of. I had to eat shit for it at school."

"Yeah, school is like that."

"I got called a queer."

"Oh."

"I'm not."

"I wouldn't care if you were."

"I'm not!"

"Okeydokey."

Then we just sat quietly for a long time. It was starting to get dusky. It gets dusky fast in the city, inside that maze of tall buildings. I felt like I could just sit there and watch the light get dim.

"And the worst part is," I said, "I have no friends at school. Not one. I've been there one whole day, and I don't know anybody. Days like this, it sucks to have no friends."

Which was a very weird thing for me to say, because I'm not a huge fan of people, and I usually prefer being alone over spending time with people, unless I know them really well or unless I've known them for a long time.

I guess I'm one of those people who don't make friends all that easily. My best friend in middle school, Rachel, once got me a shirt that said DOESN'T PLAY WELL WITH OTHERS. But I never wore it. Because it was too true to be funny.

"This might be a stupid thing to say," Frank said. "I know you're talking about friends your own age. So I hardly qualify. But if you ever get so desperate for a friend that even an old guy starts looking good to you . . . I'm a good listener."

A good listener. What a concept. That idea was so foreign to me that I just sat a minute, trying to picture how that would go. We definitely never kept any good listeners around my house. My old one, I mean.

"Thanks," I said. "I may actually take you up on that. I mean, stranger things have happened."

"So, listen," he said. "Is your kitchen unpacked yet? I mean, could you even find a fork if you needed one?"

"I thought I'd go to the deli later."

"Molly just made a batch of her homemade chicken noodle soup. You're welcome to some. You can eat with us, or I'll just bring you over a bowl. Whatever you want."

Ah. So that was the other half of "we." A woman named Molly. I'd been kind of thinking maybe Frank was gay. Something about the gentleness of him. Sort of the opposite of macho. That and the way that he was so quick to tell me he would be okay with *me* being gay. But back to the issue of this invitation at hand. I really wanted to say no. But I really love homemade chicken noodle soup. My grandmother used to make it before she died. I hadn't had food like that for years. Mother made food like shrimp cocktail or chilled soups.

"Does she even make the noodles from scratch?"

"Yup. Even the noodles."

"I'll be right over."

Molly made her homemade chicken soup with whole-wheat noodles. I wasn't used to that. But it was good. It had lots of big chunks of chicken and fresh tomatoes and big pieces of vegetables, almost like a stew.

"The thing that sucks the most," I said, "is that Donald totally knows when my birthday is. And Mother knows he knows. So it's this really stupid game. Choose me over your own daughter. And he keeps winning. That's why I'm even here."

"What do you mean?" Molly asked.

Molly was a throwback to the sixties. She had black hair in a long braid down her back like some kind of Native American princess. She wore purple. She was plump. Mother would disapprove.

I think part of me was *trying* to disapprove. I wanted not to like Molly for some reason. But it was hard. She was like Frank in that way. Someone you just almost had to like. You had no grounds not to. And it's not like me to be looking for reasons to disapprove of someone, so I had no idea what was up with that. For the moment, I just chalked it up to my generally stressed and foul mood.

But now, looking back, I think part of me might have been

just the tiniest bit aware of the fact that I was jealous of her. Because she got to live with Frank. And I didn't. But I'm sure I would have argued strenuously if you'd tried to tell me that at the time.

"Donald basically just said to Mother, 'I don't want a teenager around. Choose.' And I'm here. So we all know who she chose."

"Wow," Frank said. "That had to hurt."

I preferred to think of it as infuriating. Hurtful was a whole other ball game.

We all ate in silence for a long time.

The soup was so damn good it hurt me to scrape the last of it out of the bowl. I felt like I could eat it all day long. Like I'd been starving.

I hadn't eaten in so long. I mean, really eaten. I'd nibbled. The food was making me feel more grounded.

I said, "Would it be tacky to ask for seconds?"

"Are you kidding?" Molly said. "It's the highest compliment. Besides, you're so skinny. We need to put some meat on those bones."

Frank and Molly had two tabby cats, George and Gracie. They both rubbed against my legs at once. I wished my cat would do that. I reached down and picked one up and held him tight. Or her. I didn't know if I had George or Gracie. I didn't care. I loved friendly cats.

"Well, at least you were eighteen," Frank said. Then I just waited to see if he was smart enough to figure it out on his own. "Hey. Wait a second. Your birthday is next week? Your mother said you just *had* a birthday."

Bingo.

"That was a little white lie," I said. "It's next week. I'll be sixteen."

In the silence that followed, I watched them look at each other. I think I learned a lot from that look.

It's not like I didn't know that it's pretty radical to dump a kid in her own apartment at barely age sixteen. I knew. But my mother insisted on acting like it was no big deal. And even though I didn't believe her, I saw it all over again through Frank's and Molly's eyes. It was a pretty dicey thing to do.

I felt vindicated.

Also scared.

"That's not even legal," Molly said.

That scared me even more.

"Oh, God, please. Don't say anything. Don't get Child Protective Services in on this. Please. That's about the only way this could get worse."

"But you have to have someone looking after you."

Frank hadn't spoken yet. I was waiting to hear what he would say.

"She'll look in on me," I said.

"From the other side of town? That's criminal!" Molly had a highly developed sense of outrage. I could tell. She wanted life to be fair. I think I'd given up on that.

"*We'll* look after her," Frank said.

It was the sweetest, nicest, most wonderful thing anybody had ever said to me. It was the closest thing to open, unguarded caring that had ever been thrown my way.

I could have kissed him.

Then I sat a minute, wondering which left field that weird thought had come from.

And then I did something I don't do every day. I said thank you like I really meant it. Because I really did.

THREE

The Heartbreak of Too Many Guys Named Bob

When I woke up the next morning, Toto was up on the bed with me. As far from me as he could possibly get, but up on the bed.

And get this: he was purring.

Not at anybody or anything in particular. Just huddled there with his front legs all tucked under him, purring.

Then I thought about Frank.

Or maybe it would be better to say I *felt* about him. Felt something. Something weird.

But that little uneasy something was probably just about school looming. The Frank thing was fine. He was my friend. A nice new friend. I really liked him, sure. Who wouldn't? But just as a friend. Anything else would be pointless and stupid. And completely embarrassing.

So that's what I felt. Exactly what I said I felt.

I just really liked Frank as a friend.

Toto was still sitting there purring. I reached out to touch him. Or, I guess this would be a more accurate way to put it: I gave my hand a nerve signal to move, and before it even could, Toto sensed what was coming and split.

I just lay there, thinking, Well, that was nice while it lasted.

After that, I stuck my head out the window a lot, to see if Frank was sitting out on the fire escape. But he had school four nights a week.

Molly said he was working as a veterinary technician all day and then going to school to be a veterinarian at night. I ran into her in the hall one day, and she told me that. She said it would take him a long time.

I took it kind of hard. Hearing that he wasn't around much. But then again, I don't have tons and tons of friends. And only one ever offered to look after me. Even my mother isn't entirely committed to that.

It took me five days to find him out there.

When I did, I crawled out.

"Hey, kiddo," he said.

"Hi, Frank."

Then I felt kind of awkward and couldn't think what to say.

We just sat quietly for a while.

It was a Sunday, late afternoon, and still mostly light. The light was just barely starting to fade. The traffic was pretty thin, being the weekend. But you could still always hear sirens. Always. That's one thing you can count on in the city. There will always be some disaster going on somewhere.

Right underneath us on the street, there was some kind of

trouble going on. Some guy in a raggedy old trench coat running around yelling at everybody. Telling them to get off his street. If they didn't go, he'd run at them, waving his arms like a madman, and then they'd get scared and run away.

Frank and I just sat and watched this for a while.

"Who is that guy?" I asked. "Do you know?"

"Oh, yeah. We all know him. His name is Harry. The neighbors call him Crazy Harry. He's not exactly crazy, though. He has schizophrenia. So long as he takes his meds, he's fine. But sometimes he stops taking them. I don't know why. I guess nobody really knows why. I think a lot of people who need to be on psych meds do that from time to time. But I'm not sure anybody really knows why. Then he's all different. When he's off his meds, he never washes himself, and then after a while he starts thinking he owns the street. Then some family member or social worker or somebody comes by and gets him back on his meds. Then he's just the nicest, quietest neighbor you could possibly want. For months."

"Is he a homeless guy?"

"No, he lives in that rent-controlled building across the street. If you saw him when he was on his meds, you wouldn't think he was homeless. He looks clean. Normal, just like anybody else."

We were quiet for a little while longer, watching Harry chase people off his street.

"How's the cat getting along?" Frank asked.

"Well, better. I guess. For him, anyway. But, better for Toto is still pretty lame."

"Toto, huh?"

"Oh, right. I didn't tell you what I named him."

"Interesting choice," he said.

"Long story," I said.

We sat there for a few minutes longer, each on our own little piece of fire escape. It was getting dusky now, the time I like best in the city.

Crazy Harry was running up and down the empty street, making sure none of the people he'd chased off could sneak back again.

I had a really bad feeling that I was beginning to know why I suddenly felt so awkward and strange and tongue-tied with Frank. Even more horrifying, I thought Frank might know, too. In fact, I had this disturbing thought that Frank might have known longer than I had. Maybe I was crazy to imagine that. But I don't think so. Somehow, I think it was true. That it was just right there, lying on the fire escape in front of us, and anybody with eyes could see it.

I hoped I was wrong.

After an agonizing silence, I said, "Frank?"

But then I had no idea what I was going to say. Maybe something like, If this gets awkward, I just don't think I'll be able to stand it. Like I already couldn't cope with my life if he were not my friend.

But I couldn't say any of that. Besides, it already was awkward.

So I said, "Do you and Molly play Scrabble?"

Stupid, I know. But probably not as stupid as all that other shit I didn't say.

"I play Scrabble," he said. "I like to play better than Molly does. But I warn you. I'm pretty good."

"Okay," I said. "I'll consider myself warned."

Then he said good night and climbed back inside. And I just

kept sitting there. Trying to climb out of the way I felt. Trying to get out of myself, like I was a bad-fitting suit I could just peel away.

I guess it goes without saying that it's never that easy.

After an hour or so, Crazy Harry gave up and went back inside.

And then so did I.

At school the next day, I ran into that girl with the blue hair again. Walking down the hall. It was the start of lunch period, and I had this little carton of cut fruit in my hand, from the deli. Just like I did every day.

I'd brought lunch with me every day since my first day of school. Since the horrible locker incident. Because that way I didn't have to step foot in the cafeteria. I just sat on the stairs in an empty piece of stairwell and ate by myself.

Anyway, I was still sort of walking next to the blue-haired girl. Because, you know. Once you say "Hey," and she says it back, and you seem to be walking in the same direction, well . . . it just sort of turns into walking together.

"I don't even know your name," I said. And then I felt pretty stupid, because why would I know it? I hadn't asked her name and I hadn't told her mine. "I guess I never really introduced myself. Elle."

"As in the magazine?"

"As in Ellen. Which I totally don't relate to."

"Oh," she said. Then, just as I thought she might not be planning on saying any more, she said, "Shane."

Which sort of surprised me. "As in the boy's name?" One of

those statements you wish you could grab on their way out of your mouth. Hook them and drag them back in before it's too late. But of course you can't. It's just too late.

"There are girls named Shane."

"There are?"

"Yeah. I've known at least two."

"Oh. Okay. Sorry. My mistake. I guess I've led a sheltered life."

"Unfortunately, so did my parents. So they were totally not cool enough to name me Shane. So they pathetically named me Larissa," she said. "Which I totally don't relate to."

By this time, I'd gotten a bit distracted by the conversation. When I looked up, I saw the door to the cafeteria. The door I'd never planned to go through. We were headed right for it.

I stopped dead.

She stopped with me, and waited a minute. There was something a little different about Shane. Different how, that might be hard to say. Like she just waited sometimes. Like she knew there was something to ask, but she'd just let some silence fall before she asked it. Like sometimes she didn't really bother to talk much at all. I wasn't used to that. I was used to people who were constantly filling the air with sound.

"Not going to lunch?" she asked after a bit.

"Not sure," I said.

"You could sit with *us*."

I wasn't sure exactly who "Us" was. But somehow, with all the empty apartments, and cats that wouldn't come near me, and solitary lunches in empty stairwells, "Us" sounded like a step in the right direction.

I was getting tired of just "me."

"That would be very nice," I said. "Thanks."

There were two boys at an otherwise empty table when we sat down.

"This is Bob," Shane said, exaggerating the formality of the introduction, "and his boyfriend, Bob. Bobs, this is Elle. She's not gay. Don't get that wrong. Get that straight up front. She's a little sensitive about that."

"Bob and Bob?" I asked. "Seriously?"

One Bob was a big guy. Probably six feet or so, with these really big bones. Huge wrists and hands. A big nose. Sandy hair falling into his eyes. Bob number two was small and slight and blond, and a little more obviously gay. He had bad skin. Teenage acne. But he managed to be good-looking in spite of it.

Little Bob said, "It's really Bob and Bobby. I go by Bobby now. For obvious reasons. Shane just thinks it's funny to introduce us like that."

Big Bob said, "Shane should be careful of that thing where she has a laugh about other people's names. Since it's only out of the goodness of our hearts that we don't still call her Larissa."

I found myself glancing over my shoulder a little too much. In case there was any trouble back there. Anything I should know about. I think they all noticed. But they didn't comment.

After a few minutes of that, another guy sat down. He was a little on the tall side, taller than me, but really willowy thin. Jet-black hair, short on the sides but kind of long and poufy on top. He had a soft, very gentle face, and I noticed right away that he always looked down. Never right at anybody. And he was wearing a stretchy tank top. And eye makeup.

Shane said, "Elle, Wilbur. Wilbur, Elle."

"No, seriously," I said. Because I just assumed Shane was playing games with names again. Because nobody was really named Wilbur. Right? But in the silence that followed, I gathered that this guy really was. "Okay. Sorry," I said. "Wow. I do have a special talent for sticking my foot in it. Don't I?"

Wilbur said nothing. But I got the impression that Wilbur usually didn't say much.

The awkwardness held steady for a couple of silent minutes, then gradually faded.

Shane looked at my little plastic cup of mixed fruit. "Is that the whole lunch?"

"I guess."

"That explains why you're so thin. Hey. Where's Annabel?"

Bobby said, "She skipped out on lunch to go sit in a study hall and stare at that boy she's got the big crush on. What's his name?"

Shane said, "I no longer bother to keep track."

I was making mental notes. Or rather, editing my mental notes. I had assumed that all of the "Us" people had sexual preference in common. Except me. If I even classified as part of "Us" at this point.

I saw Wilbur glance up at me, and then away again before our eyes could meet.

Bobby said, "Okay. Enough small talk. Your story."

"What story?"

"You know. The story. The background. Around here, we begin our stories with parental status. That is, whether you live in an unbroken home, or with one parent. That sort of thing."

"Neither of the above," I said.

I had begun to abandon looking around for trouble. Looking

over my shoulder. I guess if there was trouble, it would have found us by now.

"Ah," Bobby said. "Third category. You live with an extended relative."

"Nope." Silence. I supposed they were getting tired of guessing. "I live alone."

Three out of four jaws dropped. Literally. Both Bobs and Shane actually opened their mouths and kept them that way. Wilbur just kept looking at the table.

A long, reverent silence.

Big Bob said, "It's like a beautiful recurring dream I have."

I said, "It's not as much fun as it sounds."

Little Bobby said, "I would kill to trade places with you. Seriously."

I said, "It's one of those things that look better from the outside."

Shane said, "Does anyone else besides me smell a party?"

I said, "I'm going to have to think about that."

Wilbur said nothing at all.

The first time I played Scrabble with Frank, he spelled the word "quixotic." I nearly died. The *q* was on a double-letter square, so that was worth 20, which made a 36-point word. Plus the whole thing stretched out to hit a triple-word square, so that's 108. Plus he used up all seven of his letters, and you get 50 extra points for that. So, by the time he was done, that turn was worth 158 points.

I couldn't believe it. My head was spinning. There have been times when I haven't managed to rack up 158 points in a whole game.

"A lot of it is luck," he said. "I just happened to get the letters."

"What does it mean?"

"Quixotic?" He pronounced it like it started with the word "quicks." I wouldn't have known how to pronounce it. "It comes from the legend of Don Quixote. It means fanciful, like the visions of the windmills he fought in his head."

"If it's after Don Quixote, why isn't it pronounced 'key-oh-tic'?"

"Damn good question."

Molly brought us a plate of organic fruit for the third time in less than one game. She said people didn't eat enough fresh fruit. This time it was a mango, with the pit cut out, sliced into eight long strips. They still had the peel on. I imitated Frank, eating a piece by scraping the flesh away from the peel with my teeth.

"I'm starting to make some friends at school," I said.

"Good for you," Frank said. "I know you need that."

Which is funny, because I hadn't known I needed that. Well, I don't know. Maybe I did. Maybe part of me did. And then another part of me, not so much.

"Thing is, they're all pretty much gay. Except this one girl I haven't met yet. So, now I'm sort of worried, like . . . I mean, I like them and all. But if I keep hanging out with them, then everybody will totally think I'm gay. I mean, even more than they already do."

I saw Molly and Frank exchange a quick look.

Frank finished chewing a bite of mango. Then he said, "Does it really matter what other people think? I mean, you know who and what you are. Right?"

But see, that was just the thing. That was the actual problem. Right there. Only, part of me hadn't wanted to admit it was the problem. Until the moment he said that. But then, when I didn't answer, it was kind of obvious that he had hit on something.

"Yeah, I guess so," I said.

And we played a few more rounds. A few words each. I didn't really have the right letters and I couldn't concentrate much. So the game wasn't going well on my end.

Molly was out of the room by then. And I guess I was starting to think of Frank as somebody I could talk to. Or at least, I wanted him to be. And I think I was wanting to push a little harder at my friendship with him. So we could talk on a different level.

So I said, "I really don't think I'm gay. I mean, I know I'm not now. But up until recently, I was a little freaked out about it. Because when I was, like, twelve, I had this crush on my math teacher. Mrs. Harman. Not that anything like that has happened since."

"Oh, Elle," Frank said. I thought he was going to say, You are in such denial. "Oh, honey, that is so universal."

"It is?"

"Yeah. All kids go through a stage like that. That's why when people really *are* gay, they tell their parents, and their parents say it's just a stage, and they'll grow out of it. Because that's how it is for most people. Is that all that was worrying you?"

I felt about twenty pounds lighter.

"Well, not worrying me. Exactly. But I guess when that thing happened with the locker, it sort of brought all that up again. Just that little shadow of a doubt. You know? But I know I'm not, anyway. I know that now."

Then I decided to shut up fast, before he asked me how I

knew. Why I was suddenly so sure. Because there was no good way to answer that question in front of Frank. I was steering us into dangerous territory.

I guess it was too late not to admit it. If I were gay, I couldn't possibly like being around Frank as much as I did.

Sometimes you want not to know something but it's so right in your face. It would just be pathetic to keep pretending.

Just then Molly came back into the room. And that shifted the conversation into more of a small-talky kind of territory. Because I didn't know Molly as well. I didn't even want to.

"You see how he's kicking my butt here?" I asked Molly.

"Frank is good with words."

"Words are important," Frank said. "Words are the tools we use for making peace with the world."

I lost that game by almost two hundred points.

Then again, I can't say I wasn't warned.

On my birthday, I got home from school to find a bag sitting in front of my door. One of those big paper shopping bags with the cord handles. Inside was a box wrapped in gift paper, and a clear-plastic restaurant take-out container with an enormous slice of chocolate cake. Maybe it was two slices of cake, with no slice in between. It had dark chocolate frosting and curls of shaved chocolate on top, and beside it were a bunch of candles and a cardboard book of matches.

I brought the bag inside.

I figured my mother had someone courier it over, so she could feel good about herself while sunning on the main deck in the Caribbean.

I opened the card.

"Elle," it said. "You can come over if you want us to sing 'Happy Birthday,' but we're lousy singers. Be forewarned. Your neighbors, Molly and Frank."

Then I didn't know what to feel about that. I wanted to feel like it was precious and important because it was from Frank. But it wasn't, really. It was from Molly and Frank. Which made it sort of a whole different thing.

I opened the cake box and counted the candles. Sixteen. I stuck them in the cake one by one.

Then I opened the present.

It was a stuffed cat. It was creamy white, with longish fur, and satin on the inside of its ears. It was kind of dumb, but sweet. I thought, That's a nice idea, anyway. A cat I can hug. But it's just a bunch of stuffing. I'm not really going to hug a stuffed animal. I'm really just going to say thanks and throw it in the corner.

Then I pulled it in close and hugged it. And I started to cry. Not just get teary. Really cry. It was like the dam broke. I cried all over my stuffed cat.

I didn't even know if I had Kleenex, so I had to blow my nose on toilet paper.

I lit the candles and blew them out. But I didn't know what to wish for. I had no idea what I wanted. I just knew this wasn't it.

I went to bed early, hugging my stuffed cat.

Happy birthday to me.

FOUR

I Don't Even Know What a Trans Man Is

I woke up in the middle of the night that night, and Toto was rubbing all over me. Rubbing up against my back, and then my shoulder, and then my face. First with his head, and then all the way down the side of his body, like he was just desperate to get through to somebody.

Anybody.

I held really still, because I knew the first time I moved any muscle at all, he'd be gone.

Poor Toto, I thought. You really want to be friends. I know you do. You're just too scared to do anything about it. You just can't admit, in the hard light of day, how much you need somebody.

"Poor Toto," I said out loud. I hadn't meant to say it out loud.

He skittered off the bed. I heard him hit the bedroom floor, and I lay there listening to his little kitty footsteps galloping away.

* * *

When I got to school that day, The Bobs were waiting for me at my locker. Smiling too widely. For some weird reason, I got this immediate hit that they were going to ask me a favor. Not that I'm psychic or anything. I'm totally not. But you could just sort of smell the setup.

"Hey," Bob said.

"Hey," I said.

"Hey," Bobby said.

"Hey yet again." An awkward silence. After which I said, "Well, now, why not just spit it out? Whatever it is. Just get it off your chest."

I was being slightly sarcastic. But not in a mean way. I liked The Bobs. And I think they knew it. I got the sense that they looked right through my crusty exterior to the part of me that enjoyed their company. It made me uneasy, but oh well.

"Okay," Bobby said. "It's like this." I was gathering that Bobby—Little Bob—was pretty much the spokesman. The guy who considered himself longer on people skills. "We totally understand why that party idea sort of scared you. Probably you were picturing, like, two hundred rowdy teenagers trashing your place. But we don't even know two hundred kids. We know, like . . . us. You know. Shane and Wilbur and Annabel and us and now you. So, that's all it would be. Just us. Just sort of putting on a little music and maybe drinking a beer and hanging out. Very mellow."

They had these looks on their faces. Like they were watching a teacher grade an important test that they knew they might've flunked.

"Of course," I said. "Of course you guys can come over.

Anytime. I'm really sorry if that came off wrong. That 'I need to think about it' thing. I have no idea why I always do that. I act like I don't really want friends. Or need them. And I have no idea why." And suddenly I found myself noticing more than ever that these guys were good candidates in that department. Something almost suspiciously like gratitude. For The Bobs. Don't tell anybody.

They looked at each other briefly, their faces changing. Like a dam breaking and spilling out pure joy. Big Bob spoke up for a change. "That is so cool. Thank you. We just don't have that many places we can go. You know?"

Bobby said, "Bob's parents are total, insane homophobes, and my mother is so weird she just hovers the whole time anybody is over, or actually even when I'm home alone, really. There's just no privacy. We just never get any privacy."

Wow. The Bobs totally cared for each other. Young love.

Just for a moment, I was hit with a deep pang of envy.

I said, "I'm sorry if I ever acted like it wasn't a good idea. I'm just not long on people skills, you know? And I don't usually have tons of company over. But, anyway, a party is a good thing."

I wrote down my address.

Shane caught up with me in the hall about two minutes later. Before I could even navigate between the big-talk-about-the-small-party and my first class.

She caught up with me from behind and said, "Well, the world is certainly filled with smiling Bobs this morning, isn't it?"

"Word travels," I said.

"That was very nice of you," she said.

"Occasionally I can be nice. Usually when caught off guard."

She let that one go by. "Nice to know you're not phobic when it comes to the homo of others," she said.

"I'm not homophobic at all. About anybody."

"Okay. Fine."

"I'm really not."

"Okay. If you say so, I believe you."

"I was just a little thrown by that locker thing, because I had this tiny little seed of a doubt myself. But it turned out to be nothing. Just this normal little thing that happens to practically everybody. Besides, there's this guy . . ." But I didn't even know how to finish the sentence.

"Ah. Are we in love?"

"No. It's not that big a deal."

"In lust?"

"It's not quite like that."

"A crush?"

"I don't really like that word."

"Deep admiration with some attraction thrown in?"

"Yeah. Okay. Somewhere right around in there."

By now we were standing in front of my first class. Which was not Shane's first class. I just hung there for a moment, wondering when she would move on. The conversation was making me a little uncomfortable. I was wishing the bell would ring.

"So," she said. "Anybody I know? Anybody you'll be inviting to this small get-together?"

"No. No and no. It's not like a thing that . . . It's not somebody I'm going to be with or anything. It's not like that. It's"—what was the word I was searching for?—"impossible. I only even brought it up because I just wanted you to know I'm feeling less sensitive. You know."

Then we stood there for a moment, waiting for the bell to ring. And it struck me that I was so obviously saying I was relieved to know I wasn't gay. Like that would be so awful. But I couldn't quite think how to talk my way out of it again. Honestly. Because I *was* relieved. That was just the truth.

"So, when's the party?" she asked.

And, just on that note, the bell rang.

"From the looks on The Bobs' faces, I would say very soon."

The party was set for Saturday night at eight o'clock. But The Bobs showed up at a few minutes to seven. Somehow that didn't entirely surprise me.

They brought two six-packs of beer, which they loaded into my fridge as though they had been rattling around my kitchen every day of their lives.

Then Big Bob pulled me aside, into the hall, and gave me three ten-dollar bills.

"We weren't sure what you wanted in the way of munchies," he said. "So the best thing seemed to be if we just had you run out and buy whatever you want."

"Oh. Okay. Thanks." But it seemed weird to just think of walking out of your own place when you had company. New company, particularly. "Or I could just write down a few things."

I looked up into his face, and it was just pleading. I can't think of any other word to describe it. He reminded me of a starving dog begging at the table.

"Right," I said. "Probably better if I pick stuff out myself. This should probably take at least half an hour. Maybe even forty-five minutes."

He surprised me with a kiss on the cheek. "You're the best," he said. "The absolute best. If you ever need a favor, you know who you can come to."

"It's not a big deal," I said.

But it sort of was. I guess.

I mean, it was my apartment. But I couldn't really think what it would hurt. It felt a little funny. But there was just no real reason not to cut them a break.

"It is. You know it is. Hey, be careful on your way out. There's some crazy guy out there yelling at people and trying to chase them off the street. If you don't run, he doesn't really do anything. But it seems like just about everybody runs."

"Oh. That's just Crazy Harry."

"You know him?"

"Sure. Everybody in the neighborhood knows him."

I didn't know him. Not really. But in some weird way I couldn't quite understand or explain, it made me feel closer to Frank to say that.

The rest of the gang came all at once at a little after eight. Shane and Wilbur and Annabel.

I took one look at Annabel and missed a breath. More than half of her face was a strawberry birthmark. At least, I think that's what you call it. Or a wine birthmark. And it struck me as sad, because I think she would have been really pretty without it. But it was just one of those things. You want to focus off it. You want to be one of those people who don't care. And I *didn't* care. Really. I mean, what difference would it make to me what Annabel's face looked like? I didn't even know her, and I could be friends with her either way. But it was one of those things your eye just keeps going back to. You try not to look. But then next thing you know, you're looking again.

Shane said, "Wow. The Bobs sure look happy. What's the deal with the weird guy who thinks this is his street?"

"Oh. That's just Crazy Harry. He must be off his meds again."

"We flashed Wilbur's pepper spray and he backed right off. We got the distinct impression that Crazy Man knew exactly what it was. No doubt he's had the pepper-spray experience."

I showed them into the kitchen, and they helped themselves to beers from the fridge.

"You carry pepper spray?"

Wilbur, who uncharacteristically seemed to be wearing no makeup, characteristically did not answer.

Shane said, "Always. Why do you think nobody ever gives him any shit at school? Hey. How do you feel about people smoking in your place?"

"Not good at all. But I'm fine with people smoking on my fire escape."

"That's reasonable, I guess."

Annabel kept looking up and catching me looking at her. I was relieved when she climbed out onto the fire escape with Shane.

The Bobs pretty much just sat on the couch smiling at each other while Wilbur locked himself in my bathroom. I heard Toto's claws scrambling over the hardwood floor.

That left me pretty much alone.

But, in another way, not really. I mean, not as alone as I usually was. I got myself some tortilla chips and a beer.

When Wilbur reemerged, he was wearing even more makeup

than usual. He actually looked nice. Not boy pretty or girl pretty. Just pretty.

"Sorry I scared your cat," he said.

"Everything pretty much does."

He went straight for the jade sword I had hanging over my bookshelf. Asked my permission to touch it. Take it down. It was from China. My real father gave it to me. Ages ago.

He began fencing with it, like it was a dueling sword or a light saber. Battling some invisible opponent.

Bobby said, "That would take care of your stepfather."

I think he meant it as an encouraging thing to say. But Wilbur just stopped battling and put the sword back up on its rack.

He sat quietly after that.

Then Shane and Annabel came back in, and we just all talked. I tried not to look at Annabel's face, but now and then I did. And she always noticed.

It was a weird sort of a party. I guess. I mean, I don't know. Maybe not. Maybe if a party is too normal, that's not a good thing. Anyway, it was a party. Better than any I'd ever had at my place before.

I think it was about an hour later when we got a knock on the door. Which was potentially slightly weird. Because we were all six in attendance. Everybody kind of looked at everybody else.

I answered the door and it was Frank.

I was really happy to see him. Because it seemed kind of cool for him to drop in and see me having a party with a bunch of friends. And it was kind of cool for them to see that I had adult friends who dropped by.

The whole thing just seemed unusually cool.

"Hey," he said. "Oh. Sorry. Didn't know you had company."

"Totally okay," I said. "Totally. Come in."

He stood in the middle of my living room, and everybody looked at everybody else.

It struck me that we were drinking beer. And Frank might disapprove of that. Seeing as we were all underage. Not that I ever thought he would tell me what to do or rat me out to my mother or anything like that. I just didn't want to do anything that would cause him to respect me less.

But if he had thoughts about the beer, he didn't share them. Verbally or otherwise.

"You guys were so quiet. I didn't even know you were having a party."

"Little party," I said.

"That's great that you decided to celebrate your birthday."

Shane said, "You didn't tell us it was your birthday."

"It's not."

"Well, close," Frank said. "Only a few days late."

I wanted to change the subject, so I introduced him around. First to The Bobs, then Shane, then Wilbur. Then Annabel, who I still didn't really feel like I knew at all. Wilbur looked Frank right in the eye when I introduced them. I thought that was interesting. I didn't know what to make of it. But it was interesting.

"Molly asked me to come by. She wanted me to announce in advance that tomorrow is homemade-chicken-noodle-soup night. She says she'll make an extra-big batch if you're definitely coming by."

"I'm definitely coming by."

"Good. It's a date, then. Tomorrow afternoon about six. I'll let you guys get back to your party."

I was feeling so happy that he had come by. It was all I could do to keep from smiling too widely the whole time I was walking him to the door.

But then, the minute Frank walked out the door, something very weird and bad happened. And it really caught me off guard. Because I was feeling completely relaxed with those guys. Not anticipating any trouble.

The Bobs looked at each other. Then at Shane.

Little Bobby said, "Are you thinking what I'm thinking?"

Shane said, "Probably, yeah."

Big Bob said, "Could be. Could just be."

"What?" I asked. "What are you thinking?" I could tell it was something about Frank. Just by the timing. And their faces and voices were making me uncomfortable.

Little Bobby said, "FTM."

Big Bob said, "How sure are you?"

"Seventy percent. At least."

"I'd go eighty-five," Shane said.

"What are you talking about?" I asked. My irritation sounded much more evident than I was hoping. "I don't even know what FTM is."

"Trans man," Shane said.

Annabel was in the kitchen or the bathroom. Or somewhere. Wilbur looked at the hardwood floor and said nothing at all.

"Could somebody please speak English?"

"Transgender," Bobby said. "Female to male."

My stomach burned in a weird way. I could hear my own pulse in my ears. "Are you talking about Frank?"

"That guy who was just here. Yeah. Pretty sure."

"Then I think you need to leave."

It came out sounding smooth. Cool. Not huffy or out of control at all. Like I'd just suddenly made up my mind and then the words said themselves.

They all looked at me. Shocked. Even Wilbur looked up. Full-on surprise.

Little Bobby immediately tried to smooth it over. "Elle, we didn't mean it like . . . It's not an insult. We weren't saying anything bad about the guy."

"Really. I think it would be best if you all went home."

Annabel showed up just in time to hear that remark. She stopped and stood very still. Her face an absolute blank. Obviously wondering how things could have taken such a sudden wrong turn in her relatively brief absence.

Shane said, "Elle. Coming from us, that's practically a compliment."

I didn't answer her. I was done with her. I was done with all of them. I didn't even want to deal with them while they were gathering up to go. So I just crawled out on the fire escape. As far as I was concerned, the party was officially over.

I could hear their voices inside. Saying stuff like Maybe we should go talk to her. And Does she really want us to leave? And then also some slightly more indignant things, like Where does she get off acting like FTM is an insult? And Why do we keep apologizing? We didn't do a damn thing wrong.

I heard Bobby say, "When she acts like she doesn't want friends, she's a good actor. Maybe we should just believe it."

And some much quieter mumblings from Shane, which I didn't like, even though I missed about every other word. But it was something like Can't you see what's going on? and that she'd explain it later. Which made me feel much better about the fact that I wouldn't be seeing them again.

After a few minutes, it seemed quieter. I was trying to figure out if they were all really gone when Wilbur climbed out on the fire escape with me.

"Hey," he said.

"Hey," I said. I didn't mind his being there so much. Because he hadn't said anything about Frank.

"I don't think they meant any offense by it."

"Yeah, well, it was a stupid thing to say."

We sat there for a minute in the dark, watching people and cabs go by underneath us. It was perfect for Wilbur, who always liked to look down anyway.

"Is everybody else gone?" I asked.

"Yeah."

"Did they elect you to come talk to me?"

"No. My own idea."

After a while, I decided that I needed to know where Wilbur stood on all this. In case it turned out I didn't want him sitting on my fire escape with me after all.

"Do *you* think he is?" I asked. Trying not to tip my hand and let him see how much rested on his answer.

"I don't know."

It's hard to describe the way he said it. Not like he couldn't really figure it out. Not even like he had no opinion. More like if he had a guess, he wasn't about to share it. But it didn't feel like he was just afraid of my reaction. It felt more like he declined to offer judgments about people. Which I decided was okay. I mean,

I would have liked a solid No, definitely not. But you had to respect him for that. So I let him stay.

"They weren't trying to say anything bad about your friend. I know that, because I know them. They would almost, like, have *more* respect for him if he was trans. So I guess they never thought you would see that as, like . . . a bad thing."

"I don't," I said. "I just don't think he is. And I think they should just be careful what they say about people."

"Yeah, I guess," he said. He had a weirdly soft voice. Like he was afraid to let any volume out of his mouth to touch the world. Like his voice might cause some kind of explosion on impact. But I liked that gentleness. It reminded me a little bit of Frank.

We sat and watched the traffic awhile longer. The air was starting to feel barely cool, and a light breeze had come up. I breathed as deeply as I could. I was still rattled by what had happened, and I was feeling it like a vise around my heart and lungs.

After a while, Wilbur said, "I'm gonna take off now." He came and sat closer to me. I watched in the dark as he took off something he was wearing on his wrist. A wide band of some sort. He reached his hands out.

"Give me one of your hands," he said.

I gave him my left hand, even though I didn't know why. He put the band on my wrist. Secured it with the two snaps.

"Happy birthday," he said. And kissed me on the cheek.

I looked at my wrist more closely in the light from inside. It was a wide leather bracelet made from a piece of black leather over a piece of gray leather. Both layers were cut into long, lengthwise strips, so it separated out into thin strands and it looked like you were wearing a dozen really skinny gray and black leather bracelets.

"Thank you. I really like this."

"It looks good on you." A brief, awkward silence. Then he said, "I like your friend Frank. Whatever he is."

He slipped through the window and I heard the front door close behind him.

And then I was alone. Really, completely alone.

FIVE

When Your Hair Turns Sweet Sixteen

When I showed up for homemade-chicken-noodle-soup night, Frank said, "I like your friends. They seem really nice."

"I'm not so sure anymore," I said.

"Really? I thought you liked them."

"Yeah. I guess I thought so, too. But now I'm not so sure."

"What went wrong?"

I couldn't look at him. I just kept looking down at the table. I could feel both cats rubbing against my legs. Taking turns. I wished we didn't have to talk about this. That I could change the subject.

"They just seem a little . . . judgmental."

That sat on the table for a while in silence.

Molly was dishing up soup. When she set the bowl in front of me, she said, "Were they judging *you*, honey?"

"No," I said. And I didn't say anything more.

We had all been eating for a few minutes when Frank said, "I don't know how bad it is. Because I wasn't there . . ." Yes you were,

I thought. Well, practically. "But don't be too quick to throw friends away. They can be kinda hard to replace. And then even when you get new friends, turns out *they're* not perfect, either."

You are, I was thinking. But of course I didn't say that out loud.

All I wanted was to talk about something else. So, without re-alizing I was about to, I took the conversation in a very weird new direction.

"What do you think is wrong with me?" I asked.

They were both silent for an uncomfortable length of time. I was half wishing I'd kept my damn mouth shut.

Molly spoke up first. "Why do you think anything is wrong with you?"

"Why do I fit in with them? Four of them are in that group because they're gay. So I'm not saying that's something wrong with them, but I guess it makes them different. Hard to fit in or something. Then before I met Annabel, I couldn't figure out why she hung out with them if she's not gay. But then when I met her, then I knew. So, what's wrong with me that I fit in with them but not anywhere else?"

"I don't think there's anything wrong with you," Frank said. "I don't think there's anything wrong with any of them. And I think you could probably fit in a lot of places, but I think the hair thing just got you off on the wrong foot, and I think they just happened to be the first ones who got to know you."

"I think it's because I'm not beautiful," I said. Surprising my-self yet again. I just seemed to be on a roll, spitting out things I hadn't even known I was thinking. And I was also vaguely aware that I was ignoring everything Frank had just said to me. And I'm not sure why. Because usually everything Frank said seemed important. "Sometimes I think even my own mother would love me more if I were beautiful."

"But you are beautiful," Molly said.

She said it like she really meant it. Like she believed it. I believed that she believed it. But she was still wrong.

"I'm not," I said. "I know I'm not."

"I'll prove it to you."

She got up from the table and rushed off into the bedroom and came back with an expensive-looking camera and a lot of other equipment, like some freestanding lights and a meter and stuff. She had to make several trips.

In between trips, Frank said, "Did you know that Molly is a photographic artist?"

"No. I had no idea."

I had never thought much about Molly. Never wondered who she was or what she did. Now I had this bad sense that she was taking an interest in me. And I'd have to start liking her. I knew as soon as I got to know her better, I'd have to like her. I think that's why I'd been putting it off.

"I'll show you so you can see it with your own eyes," she said, bursting back into the room. "Just be as close to yourself as you can possibly bring yourself to be."

I sat in the corner of the darkroom—their converted second bedroom—watching Molly work. On a high wooden stool, sitting on my hands. I wasn't sure what I was about to see.

"The thing to remember when you look at these," she said, "is to give up the idea that there's only one kind of beautiful. Hollywood has narrow ideas about beauty."

"So does my mother."

"Well, try to get your ideas to loosen up. Try to look at your-self the way you would look at somebody else. Imagine it's your job to hire a model. Look at these photos and see if you would hire this girl."

She started hanging wet black-and-white prints on a line, like a clothesline. I got up off my stool and felt my way over in the dim red photo light and looked at them close up.

In some of them I was looking away. I liked the angle of my jawline. It looked solid and strong. My hair being mostly gone really shifted the focus onto my face. I hated my freckles, I always had, but when I thought about this being some other girl I might hire as a model, they didn't look all that bad. On somebody else, I guess I would just think: freckles. Rather than: freckles—bad.

In one picture, I was looking right into the camera, and my eyes were so intense I almost had to look away. I stared right into my own eyes as long as I could. There was plenty going on in there. They were like a window into something that just kept going. I never knew my face showed so much of what was going on inside. I had a cute, small nose. But that wasn't even the im-portant part. It was what I saw inside those eyes.

"I *might* hire her. I'm still thinking."

"That's a start," Molly said. "You just keep thinking."

I left her in the darkroom and found Frank again in the living room. Lying on his back on the couch, his eyes half closed. I thought about how hard Molly said he worked.

"How'd that go?" he asked. He never entirely opened his eyes.

"Better than I thought it would, I guess."

I sat cross-legged on the floor next to him. He was wearing shorts and a sleeveless undershirt, and he had his arms folded behind his head. He had a lot of hair under his arms. And on his legs. And he was starting to get a five o'clock shadow. I could see the dark shape of a beard starting to form on his face.

Shane and The Bobs had no idea what they were talking about. They were just wrong. And when people are wrong, they ought to keep their damn mouths shut. If you don't know what you're saying, I think you should just stop talking.

I figured it would be best if I didn't hang out with any of those guys again. They weren't all the friends I had, anyway. I would still have Frank.

"You're my best friend," I said. Out loud.

He opened his eyes. But he didn't say anything. Or at least, not in the first couple of seconds, and then I had to plunge right in again.

"I know it sounds weird to say that."

"Why? Why is it weird?"

"Just because I haven't known you very long, I guess." Silence. Then I said, "I'm sorry if that was a dumb thing to say."

"Not at all," he said. "Just so long as I'm not your *only* friend. I think you might want to give those other kids a chance. They seemed nice to me."

"You won't be my only friend," I said.

"Good. Diversify. You owe it to yourself."

"Okay. Deal."

Notice I didn't specify who the others would be.

Maybe I could count my cat.

When I got back to my apartment, I found a very large, flat wrapped package leaning against my door. Probably as tall as my waist. Almost as wide as it was tall. Only a few inches thick. It was gift-wrapped in the world's largest piece of solid dark-green wrapping paper. It had a card stuck on with a white premade ribbon bow.

I carried it inside.

I opened the card first.

I knew in my gut it was from some or all of the people I had ejected from my place the day before. I was not particularly surprised when it turned out to be from The Bobs.

The card said:

> Elle,
>
> We are so sorry if we offended you by anything we said about your friend. We liked him a lot and did not mean the comments in any negative way. We want you to have this for your birthday. Bobby/I did it him/myself.
>
> Happy Birthday,
> Bob and Bobby

I started to try to cut the tape with my fingernail. I don't know why I do that. I feel like I should be polite to the wrapping paper while I'm opening presents. But then I just throw it away anyway.

"I guess I should just rip it, huh?" I said out loud to a perfectly empty room.

I tore off the wrapping paper to find the most beautiful painting of irises. Only three of them. Just a simple painting of three very long-stemmed flowers. I guess there's no way I can really describe it so it won't sound dumb. A painting of flowers. But they were graceful and peaceful in a way I can't really explain. And the light was hitting them in a nicely complex way.

I just stared at it for a long time.

It didn't look like a painting by somebody you knew. It looked like something you'd see hanging in a gallery. Something you couldn't afford, by an artist you didn't know and whose talent you couldn't understand.

It had a wire picture hanger on the back, with a little right-sized nail in a plastic bag taped to the wire.

After a while, I borrowed a hammer from Molly to hang it up over my couch. Unfortunately, Frank was asleep by then.

I sat on my one comfortable chair and looked at the painting. Wishing it were from somebody I wasn't mad at and hadn't just put out of my life forever. But I liked the painting so much it almost didn't matter. Well, it mattered some. But now that I'd seen the way it looked hanging over my couch, there was no going back again.

It made the place look almost like somebody's home.

Unfortunately, Frank was still asleep when I returned the hammer.

The next morning—Monday morning—I ran into Wilbur on the way to my second class.

I was glad I was wearing the leather bracelet he'd given me. I saw him glance down at it. Quickly. Then he looked me in the eye. Which I'm pretty sure he'd never done before.

"Shane's been looking for you everywhere."

"Oh," I said.

I think it was clear by the way I said it that I was not anxious to rush right off and be found.

"I think she wants to know if you guys are still friends."

"Oh."

I probably knew other words. I always had before. But none of them were coming to mind.

"If you don't want to see her, that's okay. But if you want, you could tell me where you're going to be next period. And I'll call her up and let her know."

He lightly touched the cell phone sticking up from the front pocket of his very tight jeans. A moment of silence, during which I noticed that, in addition to the usual heavy eyeliner, he was wearing green eye shadow.

It occurred to me that I was going to see her sooner or later. Maybe this was better than seeing her by surprise.

"Science," I said. "Ms. Lembecki."

He smiled a little bit. Sadly. Just with one corner of his mouth. Like he knew exactly how everything felt to me. Like he found it touching when someone else's day seemed as sad as his.

Shane was standing in front of Ms. Lembecki's room by the time I got there.

She didn't waste any time getting down to business.

"I know why you got so upset about what we said."

"I'd rather not talk about that."

"I just want you to know that a trans man is a man. I mean, in all the ways that count. Like a man who was born with this really bad birth defect. But, anyway, all I'm trying to say is that if you're attracted to him, it's the man stuff you're attracted to. It doesn't mean anything about *you*."

"He is not a trans man!" I said.

Actually, I shouted it. I really hadn't meant to shout it. The whole thing just sort of got away from me.

Every single kid within earshot—and I'm guessing there

were at least twenty of them—turned around to look. And from the looks on their faces, they all knew exactly what a trans man was.

I guess the only person to ever have not known that was me.

I only saw Annabel once. Rounding the corner in my direction as I was headed to the cafeteria for lunch. She took one look at me and stopped dead. Like she had just seen a ghost, or a glimpse of her own death or something. Then she turned and rounded the corner again, right back the way she had come.

I sat by myself in the cafeteria.

I guess I should admit the whole cafeteria thing hadn't been a well-thought-out plan. I should have gotten something at the deli and eaten by myself. As I'd headed to school that morning, I hadn't been thinking how much this would change having lunch. I hadn't thought out all the various ways in which things would be different now.

I sat alone at a corner table and watched the melee of moving bodies and listened to the racket of voices.

And watched the "Us" folks at the usual table.

And marveled at the way everybody left us alone.

Not like they accepted us exactly. More like, now that they'd labeled us, we didn't need to exist in their world. If we didn't do anything special to jump up onto their radar screens, I guess they really didn't think about us at all.

I saw Bobby glance over his shoulder at me about three times.

Finally, he got up and came in my direction. Just Little Bobby. Nobody else.

I jumped to my feet and dumped the rest of my lunch in the trash bin and tried to hurry out before he could get to me. But we just ended up meeting at the door and walking out into the hall together.

"I hope you got my present," he said.

"Yeah, I did." But it seemed really cruel to just leave it at that. I mean, since it was original artwork and all. "I like it."

"Really?"

"Yeah. I like it a lot. I hung it over my sofa. It really adds a lot to the place."

"You're not just saying that?"

"No. I really mean it. You're talented."

He looked down at the floor and away to deflect the compliment. "Bob thinks so. But, you know. I think he's prejudiced."

"Maybe. But he could also be right."

Long silence. We were still walking together. But I had no idea where we were going. I'm pretty sure he didn't, either. Lunch wasn't anywhere near over. We had no place we needed to be.

"So," he said. "Are we okay, then?"

"Yeah," I said. "Yeah. Sure."

It was both the least true and the least convincing thing I'd ever heard myself say.

When I got home from school that day, I walked into my apartment and found somebody there. Sitting at my kitchen table. I think I might have literally jumped, and I let out an embarrassing involuntary scream.

The murderous intruder jumped up and spun around.

It was only my mother.

Then she screamed, too.

"What?" I said. "It's me. Who were you expecting?" I mean, who was supposed to be surprised and invaded, anyway?

60

I watched her face gradually change. It started out afraid of me, as if I were some total stranger. But instead of the relief of recognition, her new expression was hurt and ruined, as if she were about to burst into tears.

Oh. Right. The hair.

"I thought you were getting back tomorrow," I said.

"No. Yesterday."

"I thought it was tomorrow."

"No. It was always yesterday."

I saw a stack of the usual boxes and bags on the table. Typical birthday stuff. Don't ask how I could know it was typical without opening it. But they mostly had that high-end-department-store-clothing-box look. Which was typical. She always bought me presents intended to turn me into the girl she thought I should be. Or to turn me into her. Or maybe I just said the same thing two different ways.

Before she could even assault me about the hair issue, I said, "How did you get in? Did you keep a key?"

"Of course I did. What if you were hurt or in trouble?"

"Funny. You keep saying that. But I think that whole 'hurt or in trouble' thing is the reason why most parents keep their teenagers around the house."

"Why did you do that to your hair?"

"I think you owed me the respect of telling me if you were going to keep a copy of my key."

"Was there an actual reason? Like something got stuck in it, or it got burned or something?"

"I also think you should call if you're going to come by. After all, this is my place now. You would be furious if somebody came by unannounced."

"Or were you just being willfully destructive?"

Just so you know, this was not at all unusual. This two-simultaneous-conversations thing. My mother and I did this on many an occasion.

"The latter," I said. Just to shut things down once and for all. "Next time, please call before you come. You scared me half to death."

"I just wanted to tell you all about my cruise. And plan your big birthday party. Although this changes things somewhat. I'm not sure how we'll . . . Oh wait, I know. I have a lovely cloche hat that would look like heaven on you."

"I frankly don't want to hear about the cruise. And I'm not wearing your hat. And I don't want a birthday party. Especially not now that I know that it was never really for me. It was always for my hair."

"Please don't be like that, darling. Of course we'll have a party."

"I already had one," I said.

"What?"

"I think you heard. I had a birthday party already. With my friends. And they gave me nice presents, too. A stuffed cat and this nice leather bracelet and that painting of the irises that's hanging over the couch. So, that's it. Birthday's over. You missed it. You can't just change the date of a thing like that, you know. You either care enough to be there for it or you don't."

"I think I'll just give you a little time to think this over."

"Good plan," I said.

That way she would go away. And next time she called or e-mailed, I could just tell her my feeling hadn't changed.

"Are you sure you don't—"

"What happened to my time to think this over?"

62

She sighed.

She touched my cheek once as she was leaving.

In her eyes I saw something potentially a little bit new. Like I might've really hurt her. Like maybe all of this was hurting her, maybe more than I knew. And like maybe I was making this bad thing worse for her instead of better.

Except I really don't think it's my job to make it easier for her to abandon me.

Then she looked back at my hair and the moment was lost.

After she left, I opened my presents.

I took a hard look at all the crap my mother had given me for my birthday. Shoes. A dress. A fur jacket. All stuff to wear. All stuff she would wear and I wouldn't. All stuff that would make me look just the way she wanted me to look.

Just like I expected.

Mother always wrapped the receipts with the packages, in case the size was wrong or something. And maybe, underneath that, so I'd know how much she spent. But usually I didn't exchange it. Usually I just let it rot in a drawer.

I took out all the receipts and looked at them. Totaled them up. Hundreds of dollars. And all from the same department store.

I took it all back.

I turned it all in for store credit, and then I bought a 35 mm camera, with two extra lenses—a close-up and a wide-angle—and a flash, and a tripod, and a light meter, and a book about photography.

And I carried it all home.

SIX

How to Freeze the World in One Easy Lesson

Next time I played Scrabble with Frank, I did a little better. I only lost that game by about 150 points.

"I want to hear you guys sing," I said as we were gathering up the tiles again. I think I was trying to move on to some area of life that wasn't Scrabble. I was definitely outclassed in Scrabble.

"No you don't," Frank said.

"You really don't," Molly said.

"No, I really do. After seeing how well Molly takes pictures and how well Frank plays Scrabble, now I want to see you guys do something you suck at."

"Well," Frank said. "You asked for it."

They sang, "Happy belated birthday to you." They were pretty bad. Not the worst I've ever heard, but bad enough.

"Yeah," I said. "That pretty much makes up for the Scrabble."

"We can dance, though," Frank said. "We're good dancers."

"What kind of dancing?"

"Ballroom."

"You're kidding. How weird." Then I realized I was being rude. "I don't mean weird." But it *was* weird. Really. In a way. "I just mean, like . . . you don't see that a lot anymore."

"Ballroom dancing is still very popular."

"Oh. Well, maybe not with the high school crowd. Are we talking about like Arthur Murray stuff? Like in old Fred Astaire movies?"

"Very loosely speaking."

"Can I see?"

We moved the couch back to the wall, and they put on an actual vinyl record, the kind you need an old turntable to play.

"Benny Goodman," Molly said as she set the needle down.

"Who's Benny Goodman?"

"One of the old original swing-band leaders from the thirties and forties," Frank said.

"You weren't even born then." Oh God. I hoped not. "Were you?" Then I realized how hugely dumb that was. Of course not.

"No, but I still know good music when I hear it."

The record started playing, and it was like one of those instrumental big-band songs you would hear on the soundtrack of a movie about a big World War II army dance at the USO club.

Then they danced for me.

First, it made me uncomfortable. Because the minute they started dancing, they just totally focused on each other. Totally. They were looking right into each other's eyes and smiling, and it was so clear and so real that they were a team. An old, practiced team. A team that nothing and nobody could get in the way of.

Not that I had ever planned to try. But still.

I'm not really sure why I do that. Or even how. Like when I

65

want something not to be true, I sort of feel like it isn't. Like I see this Frank-and-Molly thing on a day-to-day basis, but part of me doesn't believe it's really real.

Only, at a time like this, it is.

It's right in front of your eyes, and then you not only know it's real in that moment, you know it was all along.

The kind of thing that can ruin your whole day if you let it.

But after a while, I managed to focus off that and actually sort of enjoy watching them. Because they were good. Really good.

I mean, Frank spun Molly around and they dipped and they came together and came apart like they'd been doing it for years. I guess they'd been doing it for years.

"Can I take some pictures of you guys dancing? I think it would look cool."

Molly stopped dancing, and it was funny, because it took Frank just a moment to notice. He just sort of went on dancing a few steps without her.

"I didn't know you were into photography," she said.

"Well, I'm not. I mean, I am. But I haven't been for long. I'm not into it like you're into it. I'm just getting started."

"Film or digital?"

"Film. I had to really insist on a film camera. The guy at the store kept trying to sell me on digital. Almost everything they had was digital."

I didn't say why it was so important to me to go with film. I don't think I had to. It was this sort of difficult, embarrassing truth that was right there for everybody to see: the fact that my interest in photography probably had its roots in admiring Molly just a little bit. Whether I wanted to admire her or not. Whether I wanted to admit it or not.

I hurried up and talked over all that again.

"But I know how to use the camera I bought. I didn't just buy it and put it in the corner. I've been teaching myself how to use it."

"You should have told me. You could have asked for help. I would have helped you if I'd known."

"I was going to ask for help. I think. I mean, sometime I would have. You know. Sooner or later."

"You want to run get your camera?" she asked.

"Yeah, but . . ."

I wanted to ask something but it seemed a little gutsy. Like giving orders. Like running the show all of a sudden. But it felt like I really knew what I wanted and needed right then, so in a rare moment of pseudo-confidence, I just pushed through and said it. And it got said:

"But come over to my apartment. I want to put up some kind of backdrop, so it looks like a studio shot. And you guys need to dress up more, so it looks real formal and all. And, Frank, you need a shave."

See? I could open my mouth and just say things. And also, another moment to note that the "Us" guys were totally full of shit. Frank needed a shave.

I moved almost all the furniture out of my living room and tacked two ironed sheets to the far wall.

It was quite a production.

When Frank and Molly came over, Molly was wearing a black dress, like an evening dress, with a full skirt, and Frank was wearing a gray suit and a blue tie. I'd never seen them so dressed up before.

Frank looked so nice in a suit. Too nice, really.

Molly helped me with the lighting. She said I needed a lot of light because they would be a moving subject. So I'd need a fast shutter speed. And I had to decide between tripod and handheld. Tripod, they'd dance in and out of the frame. Handheld, I might have trouble with my composition. I told her I might try a few of each.

Then we realized we didn't have any music. They danced anyway. Molly just hummed a tune, and they danced, and I used up a whole twenty-four-exposure roll of film, and then reloaded and shot some more.

Molly gave me a tip on a good developing lab. But she promised that later on, when I was a little deeper into my learning curve, she'd help me develop a roll. Show me some of the tricks you can do when you develop your own.

When I got the pictures back, I found out I'd made a lot of mistakes. A lot of them. Photo after photo, they were half dancing out of the shot. My focus was bad a lot of the time. But I took almost fifty photos. So maybe by the law of averages, about five of them were really good.

I laid them out on my kitchen table.

Frank and Molly looked like they'd danced right off the screen of an old movie. I was so proud. I thought, I did that. Not just pointed the camera. I saw something I knew would make good photos, and I staged a photo shoot, and I got what I wanted. I saw now, on my kitchen table, what I'd seen in my head when I asked permission to shoot them.

In the best one, Molly's skirt was just a little bit blurred by the way it was spinning. Just enough that you could really feel the frozen action of the shot. And the looks on their faces were caught just right. You could see them loving dancing and loving each other. The expressions just said it all.

It was so nice to look at. I was even able to stand outside the fact that it was Molly and Frank and enjoy the look of love on their faces. Love always looks nice. I don't really know anyone who doesn't enjoy it when they see it. Anyone who doesn't, I don't really want to know them.

It was only five photos, and they were good almost by accident. But next time it wouldn't be an accident. Next time I would know a lot more.

I heard a knock at my door. I thought it was either Frank or Molly. I ran to the door because I was so happy to show them my pictures.

I threw the door open wide.

It was my mother. I think she could tell I was disappointed.

"What are you doing here?"

She looked hurt. "I came to visit you."

"I thought you were going to call first."

"I knocked. I thought you just wanted me to knock."

"Next time call first. Please?"

She sighed and swept dramatically over to my table and started looking at the photos. I really hadn't invited her to look at them. They felt a little private, in a weird way. Not that there was anything wrong with them. But there were lots of parts of my life that I wasn't anxious to share with my mother. Plus, I was really itching to go over and show them to Molly and Frank. So the whole thing was making me feel a little grumpy.

"What are these?"

"What do they look like?"

"Well, they're photos, of course, but who took them?"

"I took them."

"Using what for a camera?"

"Using my camera for a camera."

She leveled me with a disapproving look. "If you're receiving expensive gifts from someone, I should know."

"*You* bought me the camera."

"When did I do that?"

"For my birthday."

She just stood quietly a minute, and I felt like I could see wheels turning in her brain. "Oh," she said, as if someone had just defaced a Michelangelo, "all those beautiful clothes." Long, semitragic pause. "I didn't even know you were interested in photography."

"Probably because you don't know me anymore at all. Which is probably because we don't live together."

"You're being unnecessarily cruel today, Ellen. Who are these people?" She pointed to the photos.

"My next-door neighbors."

"Ah, yes. That nice little man. So you're getting friendly with them?"

"Yeah. What's wrong with that?"

"Nothing. I suppose. I just thought you'd make friends your own age."

"I have friends my own age."

I purposely neglected to mention that I was barely speaking to any of them.

I felt another one of those moments coming on. Where I knew exactly what I wanted and needed. But it was hard to say.

But I was about to say it anyway. Against all odds.

70

"Now, if you'll excuse me, I sort of have something planned. I've been learning about photography from Molly next door. And the next thing I was going to do is go over there and show her these pictures. Which is why I would really appreciate it if you'd please call first. Next time. You know. In case I have plans."

She stomped her foot suddenly on my hardwood floor.

It was unexpected. And kind of funny, actually. Like a three-year-old who can't get her way by using words.

"Elle, I think you're being very unpleasant to me."

But I really hadn't intended to be. I really hadn't said any of that to hurt her. I just wanted to go on with my day.

"No unpleasantness intended," I said. "But like it or not, I have a life now. I think maybe you thought you could have it both ways. You know, like, drop me here to live on my own and go off on a cruise with Donald first thing, and still have it be just like it was before. But it's not like it was before. It's not. In any way. And it never will be again. And I think you might just need to accept that."

I walked to the door and opened it wide.

She stormed out without a word.

I felt like I'd won a major victory. I guess in some ways I had.

I sat at the kitchen table over at Frank and Molly's, showing Molly my photos.

"These are good work," she said. "Great work for a beginner."

I could actually feel the words move down into my gut. Like a warm, tingly glow. They actually had an effect on my body.

I knew damn well that Molly didn't throw compliments around lightly, or say anything she didn't mean. Even though I hadn't really known her that long. It was just one of those evident things. It would be the first thing you would know about her, and the minute you knew it, you would be completely sure.

Frank was taking a nap on the couch, but it didn't seem like we had to worry about being quiet. I guess he was tired from working and going to school. He looked different without his glasses. He had dark circles under his eyes. He looked kind of defenseless. Which looked sweet.

It made me feel almost like I really did love him. Which, between that and the compliment on my photography, well—it was a lot to feel all at once. It almost made me a little dizzy.

I tried to pay attention to Molly and not stare at Frank while he slept.

"I made a lot of mistakes," I said. "These were the only good ones."

"You're supposed to make mistakes. You're just starting out. Mistakes are a good thing. They mean you were brave enough to try something hard."

I could feel one of their cats rub up against my legs. I picked the cat up, and held her in my arms and hugged her. It was Gracie. I loved Gracie. I loved them both.

"My cat still doesn't let me touch him," I said.

"Be patient."

"I am. I guess. I mean, there's nothing I can do about it. I still sometimes wonder why I picked him."

"Maybe because you knew how badly he needed to be picked."

"Yeah. Maybe."

"Or maybe he picked you."

"Or maybe I really was just trying to get back at my mother. I was pretty mad at her that day."

"Or maybe all of the above."

"Yeah. Maybe all of the above."

I watched Frank sleep some more, but Molly was kind of watching me watch him, and that made me uncomfortable.

"Will you show me some of your work?"

"Of course I will," she said.

She brought out a huge, flat, leather-bound portfolio. I already wanted one just like it. Even though I knew it was way too soon for me to need something like that.

They were almost all photos of people. Mostly on the street. Homeless people, working-class people. Faces in a crowd.

They all looked like they were missing something really, really important. Like she was taking pictures of the holes in people's lives.

Some looked hungry, or like they had no place they belonged. Or both. Others looked lonely. A lot of them looked lonely. Like, I guess there's a lot more lonely going on in the world than I'd really ever stopped to think about.

Some looked angry. But then, even the ones who looked angry also looked lonely or scared. Usually anger seems to be a feeling that people have all by itself, with no other feelings around it. Or under it. But not in Molly's pictures. In Molly's pictures, people felt lots of different feelings, all at the same time.

And they say the camera doesn't lie. So I knew life must really be the way it was in Molly's pictures. Which means there was a whole other layer of life I didn't even know about until I saw it in her portfolio.

That's a lot for a person with a camera to be able to do.

One of them she won an award for. A national award. It was a picket line, everyone joined together arm in arm to keep the scabs from coming through, and the faces on both sides were just so fierce. It was like Roman gladiators, except it was here, and now.

Lonely. Scared.

So, they weren't just pictures. I mean . . . what do I mean? They weren't just simple pictures whose only job is to look nice. They had something to say. They were each a sort of document of some kind of injustice. Usually people do all this shouting about injustice. But Molly's photos just froze the injustice, and then it was right there in front of you. And you couldn't look away anymore. They just presented you with the injustice and then left you to do all the rest of the work on your own. You either cared or you didn't. But you couldn't ever pretend again.

I had no idea, until that exact moment, that a camera could do so much.

I was so caught up in what they made me feel, and in all the thoughts running laps in my head, I think I actually forgot that Frank was sleeping right across the room on the couch. The whole world, just in that moment, was about the possibility of taking pictures.

For the first time ever, I knew there was something I really cared enough to do. I actually wanted to *be* something.

Then I wondered how I'd ever managed to live my life and be happy without knowing this important thing I wanted to be. Even though it had been just a matter of minutes.

Still, some minutes are longer than others.

SEVEN

I Don't Even Know What Top Surgery Is

I think it was about seven days later that I realized I hadn't seen Toto in a long time. But maybe it was nine. I should've kept better track of him, but he was always hiding someplace or another, and there's only just so much of the day you can spend on a treasure hunt for your weird cat.

He had a food dish that I checked a couple of times a day, and if I saw he was low on dry food, I filled it up. All of a sudden one lazy Sunday afternoon it hit me. It wasn't low, but it should have been. It hadn't been low for days.

I hunted.

I found Toto in the closet, nested in some dirty clothes on the floor. I didn't exactly have a hamper yet, so the bottom of the closet was temporarily filling the bill.

He looked up at me in the half-light. Looked at me with that one eye, and my stomach jerked, and I knew something was really wrong. Because he didn't run away.

I took the lamp from the bedside table and pulled it as far as the cord would stretch. Shined it in on him.

He still didn't run.

He turned his face up to me, and it wasn't shaped right at all. It was all lumpy and puffed up on one side. So much that it pushed his nose over in the other direction. So much that his one good eye was partly shut.

I just stood there for a second, not knowing what to do. The vet we used for Francis was all the way on the other side of town. And he wasn't open on Sunday anyway. And I didn't even know how to get Toto into the carrier.

Then it hit me. Frank.

I almost ran over there and asked him to help me.

But then I decided I had to at least put Toto in the carrier. I was on my own now. I didn't want to be helpless. I couldn't just rely on Frank for everything. Or maybe I wanted Frank to be proud of me for being able to handle things. I just knew that sooner or later I had to be able to handle my own cat.

I got the carrier and brought it back to the closet door.

It was easy to get him cornered in there.

I took him by the scruff of the neck. I thought, I'll do this just like Frank showed me. But I couldn't pin him to my side. I had to dangle him in the air and lower him down into the carrier. So his back legs were swinging free, and he got panicky, and I felt one set of back claws rake down the side of my wrist. Bad one, I could tell. But there was no time to think about it now.

I closed the carrier and ran over to Frank's apartment. Banged on the door. I could hear a lot of noise in there. Lots of voices. Dozens. They had people over. Multiple people. Maybe even a party.

76

Maybe I'd even heard the party before. Through the wall. And just hadn't really focused on the fact that the voices were coming from Molly and Frank's. Maybe it just didn't sink in until I was standing in front of his door. Wishing I hadn't just knocked.

I turned to run back to my own apartment. Then I froze again. I couldn't bring myself to yell for help to Frank when they were having a party. Then again, I couldn't just go home without any help for my cat.

Before I could decide whether to run away or not, Frank answered the door.

"Elle, honey, what's wrong?"

"I need your help with Toto. He's sick. But you're having a party. . . ."

Frank looked down at my hands. At the hall carpet at my feet. "He's bleeding? Where's he bleeding from?"

"No. No, he's not bleeding. No, the bleeding would be me. But he hasn't eaten for days, and his face is so swollen up that he can barely see out of his good eye. And he doesn't even run from me. Toto. Doesn't run from me. So this is really bad."

"You better come in," he said.

It felt good to have him just sort of take over. Just take me under his wing like he always did so well, and then I knew Toto and I would both be okay. It made all the scared places in my gut feel warm and settled.

Then I walked into their apartment. And then nothing felt warm and settled anymore.

I looked around at their friends. Some just looked like anybody else you'd meet. But about half a dozen of them were, like . . . I don't know any other way to say this, so I'll just say it. Like men in dresses. Like you could just see by their faces and shapes that they were men. But they were wearing makeup and women's clothes and either wearing wigs or just had their hair done up in a women's style. One of them looked really fifties old-fashioned in a high-necked dress, white gloves, and a single strand of pearls. Another was wearing jeans and a skinny spaghetti-strap tank top, but his shoulders and arms looked too big to pull it off. Then a few others were sort of in between. And a lot of the women looked really gay. And some of the men who were dressed like men were . . .

You know what? I think I kind of stopped trying to take it all in at that point. Some of them just looked and felt strange to me.

I tried to turn back to Frank. To follow him into the kitchen. He was trying to lead me into the kitchen. But he had stopped for a minute while I looked around. He looked vaguely uncomfortable.

On the way into the kitchen, I saw one other thing. One huge other thing, sitting over by the window.

It was a top surgery tree.

Not that I know what a top surgery tree is. I had no idea. But it had a sign on top that said TOP SURGERY TREE. So there you go. So that's what it was. It was like a Christmas tree but with no green needles. Only bare branches. And on the sharp ends of the bare branches people had stuck money. Twenty- and fifty- and hundred-dollar bills.

But, like I usually do with anything I have no frame of reference for, I just sort of put it out of my head again.

But the people. That stayed with me. And rattled me a little bit.

We stood at Frank's kitchen sink, and he washed my wrist off with antibacterial soap, and it stung like crazy.

"You're supposed to be entertaining your guests," I said.

"It's not a problem," he said.

He put ointment on the scratches. Four of them, the longest about three or four inches, from the side of my hand all the way up past my wrist. He brought out a box of giant-sized Band-Aid patches. It took three to cover the damn thing.

"Okay," he said. "Now we worry about the cat. We'll take him down to my work. I'll call one of the vets from my cell on the way and have somebody meet us there."

"But your company."

"It's okay," he said. "They'll get by for an hour while we're gone."

We walked fast to the subway together, and Frank held the carrier. I felt like *I* should, because Toto was my cat. But he was heavy, and it's hard to walk fast lugging an extra fifteen pounds. I could barely keep up with Frank as it was.

The street was crowded with people walking in both directions, and now and then someone wouldn't yield, and I'd get separated from Frank and Toto and have to run a few steps to catch up. Half the people who passed us were chatting on their cell phones, and people's cigarette smoke blew back and caught me in the face, and I waved it away.

I felt relieved when we trotted down the steps into the subway. I like the subway. I'm not sure why.

Right away I could feel it get cooler. It's usually cooler down there, and a little bit moist, like a cave.

I used to like to stand right by the edge of the platform and look down the tunnel, waiting to see the lights of the train. Back in the old days, when hardly anybody got pushed onto the tracks.

Without a word to each other, without any discussion of how we do these things, Frank and I took a spot with our backs up against the cool wall. I could feel the edge of an ad frame against my back. I could feel the wood of the bench we'd chosen not to sit on. It was right up against my left leg.

I thought about Frank's friends from the party, then pushed the images out of my head again. But I kept having that constant feeling like there was something I was purposely not thinking about.

When the train came, the brightness of the inside of it seemed comforting somehow.

We sat on the hard plastic seat, the cat carrier between us on the floor. I was wondering why we weren't talking.

Then I realized it was me.

I clam up when I'm upset. But realizing that didn't exactly fix it.

I just sat there, stony, watching the lights flicker off and then on again. Listening to the clatter of the metal wheels on the tracks. Feeling the rocking that is pure subway, that just doesn't feel like any other transportation in the world.

Then I said, "I should've known he was sick. What was I thinking? Letting him sit in that closet for days. I never even looked around for him."

"He's a different kind of cat," Frank said. "You expected that kind of remote behavior from him. If he came around a lot on his own, I'm sure you would have missed him when he stopped."

I wondered if that meant Frank thought it was Toto's fault. I didn't figure it could be. It was never the cat's fault. That would be like blaming a three-year-old. I was the grown-up in charge. The buck had to stop with me.

"Are you saying it was Toto's fault?"

"I'm saying there's no point blaming anyone in this case."

We sat quiet awhile longer, feeling the distinctive rocking. Comforting.

Then Frank said, "Nobody else would have taken that cat out of the pound, Elle. You know that. That cat would already be dead if it wasn't for you. You're taking the best care of him you can, and he doesn't make it easy. Can you let yourself off the hook for this?"

"Yeah," I said. "Sure. I guess."

But I was halfway lying. Telling Frank what he wanted to hear. Maybe I could let myself off the hook. Eventually. But not just like that.

Another very long silence. But this one was more strained and painful. At least for me.

"What's top surgery?" I asked.

I heard him pull in a deep breath. It was probably only a second or two before he answered. But it was the longest second or two in the history of civilization.

"It's a phase of gender-reassignment surgery." A heavy, dead weight in my stomach. A little nauseating. "It's a double mastectomy, but then also with some cosmetic surgery to give the chest more of a male shape and appearance."

"I guess it's none of my business," I said.

The words sounded like they were coming from someone else. My lips felt numb. Also my brain.

"Well, you're my friend," he said.

Which I took to mean I could ask more questions. If I wanted to. But there was only one more question I could think to ask.

I didn't want to.

*　*　*

I paced around in the waiting room for a long time. I had the whole area to myself. I read the pet cartoons on the bulletin board. Looked at the pictures on the walls. A puppy sleeping flat on his back, his belly exposed to the cool air from a fan. A cat holding a mouse, but not a real one. A computer mouse. Holding the thin cable in his teeth, the mouse hanging down in front of his chest.

There was a canister of doggie treats on the counter, with a label that said THANKS FOR BEING PATIENT.

A middle-aged woman with wildly curly hair came out from the back and stood behind the counter. The swinging door made a *whoosh* noise behind her.

"Has anyone filled you in yet, dear?"

"Oh. I'm waiting for Frank. Frank is back there with my cat."

"Right. The cat with the infected tooth."

Then I felt better, because it was just an infected tooth. How bad can that be? Right? Pull the tooth if you have to. Put the cat on antibiotics. Nobody ever died of an infected tooth. Right?

Just then Frank came out through the swinging door. *Whoosh.* I looked at his face for encouragement, but he wasn't giving anything away.

"Shirley, I'll call for an update."

I followed him out the door.

"What?" I said. "He's okay, right? It's just an infected tooth. He'll be okay, right?"

"Yeah, that's what we hope," he said.

We walked down the street together, and he steered me toward a coffeehouse.

"Wait. Don't you have to get back to your party?"

82

"In a minute. We're just going to talk for a minute."

My stomach felt like it was swarming with stinging insects. This was not going to be a good talk. I could feel that much. I could tell.

"Can't they just pull the tooth?"

"Yeah, it'll come out today. But we're a little concerned because we think he might have a secondary infection."

He held the door open for me, and the sound of people chatting and milk being steamed felt welcoming in a weird way.

"Is that serious?"

"Can be pretty serious, yes. But he's getting the best care."

"You know money is no object, right? I mean, my mother feels so guilty. No way she's going to refuse me anything now. Whatever that cat needs—"

"We're doing the best we can for him, Elle. What do you want to drink?"

I ordered a chai latte, and Frank ordered a cappuccino, and we shuffled around silently, waiting for them to come up. Then we sat at a tiny round table on uncomfortably high stools.

I blew on my chai latte and felt the hot steam come up into my face. "I guess it would have been better if I'd caught it earlier."

Frank set down his cup and sighed.

"Elle, that cat was voted least likely to ever get out of that pound on his own four paws. Do you know what the chances were that he'd end up with someone who would shout 'Money is no object!' on his behalf?" He waved his arm in the air as if he were waving a fistful of hundreds around.

I smiled in spite of myself. "I didn't do that, did I?" I imitated the money-waving gesture. I hated to think I was becoming that much like my mother.

"No, I threw that in to try to make you laugh."

I looked at the expression on his face, kind of sympathetic but sad, and I did laugh, just a little. For just a minute, I got out of myself and laughed. It had been a bad day. Still was. It felt good to laugh. Even for just a minute.

Then I said, "What are his chances?" And braced myself hard for the answer.

"Better than fifty-fifty. I think. But maybe not much better. Look. Elle. There are things we can do something about and things we can't. You figured out he was in trouble. You got him in the box. At great personal sacrifice, I might add. You got him to a good vet. Now comes the part that isn't up to you. Same with the vet. She'll do everything she knows to help him get better. But then it's out of her hands. The trick is to do what you can do and then let go. Just go home and wait. I know you'll still worry about it, but it really doesn't help to stress. Hurts you and doesn't help him. I'll let you know if anything changes. You can call me. Or come by if you want."

"Okay," I said.

But I wasn't sure how one goes about not stressing. Every time I got good advice, it felt like there was some kind of instruction sheet missing.

I thought about going by. And whether all those people would still be there.

"Not that it's any of my business," I said. I could feel my heartbeat pulsing in my ears. I felt a little dizzy. "Whose top surgery are you raising money for?"

I tried to swallow but it didn't quite work. I'd forgotten how.

It's like I had to ask sooner or later. It's like it was just going to sit there on the table like this big pink dinosaur that nobody wanted to admit was sitting there. Until I finally just took a deep breath and asked.

But I already knew. I swear I already knew. The noises of the other patrons seemed far away, like sounds do in the minutes before you fall asleep. I felt empty and dead inside from what I already knew.

"Mine," he said.

Then I just sat there and drank most of the rest of my drink and said nothing. And thought nothing. Everything just seemed heavy and dark, and I was there in the middle of it. Thinking nothing. But no matter how hard I thought nothing, I couldn't get my stomach to stop tingling.

"Why do I care about that cat?" I asked. After quite a long silence. It kind of surprised me. Who knew I was about to ask that?

"Well. He's your cat."

"Yeah, but he doesn't care about *me*. I've never even touched him. Except this morning. Which was hardly a cuddly experience." I ran my hand over the sea of big Band-Aids. It hurt. "And here I am dying inside because he might not be okay." And for other reasons I wasn't ready to go back to. "Why?"

Frank blew foam around on top of his cappuccino. "Human nature," he said. "To get attached to living things. Especially if we've made ourselves responsible for them. You just look into an animal's eyes and decide he'll be yours, already there's a bond. You feel for Toto because he needs so much help. I know it's making you hurt right now, but let me tell you, that's a part of human nature we would not want to lose. Boy, you look at how bad things are now . . . just think where we'd be if that empathy ever got lost."

Before he left to go back to his party, I thanked him for being so much help. I thought that was good that I did that.

"No problem," he said. Then he said, "I'm sorry if you're having trouble with this."

"Oh. Right," I said. Wishing we hadn't switched topics again. "Well. I guess that's not really your problem. Is it?"

"Not really," he said. "But you're my friend. So I'm sorry if this is weird for you."

Awkward silence.

"Okay. Thanks."

"I'll call you if I hear anything about the cat."

"Thanks."

This officially began the period in my life I tend to refer to as After.

After, I went home.

There was no cat at home. It shouldn't have felt all that different, to have no cat at home. If there had been, he only would have been hiding under the bed anyway. But he wasn't hiding under the bed. And he might never be hiding under the bed again. So that was different.

After, I listened as the party began to break up next door. Every time I heard laughter, it made my face burn and tingle. Don't ask me why. I guess it reminded me to picture the people next door.

After, I found I had this weird tendency to notice that the refrigerator door was open and I was standing in front of it, looking in. Every time that happened, I racked my brain trying to remember having opened the door. I knew I must have. That sort of went without saying. But there was no information available. I just woke up in that burst of cool air.

Around the third time it happened, I began to lose patience with the process. I grabbed one of the four beers left over from the party and took it out on the fire escape.

I thought I was thinking nothing. Doing nothing. My brain was in a total state of idle. But then all of a sudden I got this mental flash of Toto hiding under the bed and hissing at me when I looked in at him. With his one gold eye shining in the dark.

And I started to cry.

Fortunately, it was pitch-dark. So when Frank stuck his head out, I'm pretty sure he didn't know I was crying. At least, I hope he didn't.

"Hey, Elle. Want me to come sit out with you?"

It struck me suddenly how utterly ridiculous it is to ever think you know anybody. Or to ever think you've found anybody you can love.

Because you don't know anybody.

Ever.

Especially when you haven't even known them all that long. But, really, not even when you've known them all your life. I never thought my mother would trade me for some dork named Donald. And I sure as hell never thought Frank was anything other than a guy.

"No thanks," I said. "I was just going in anyway."

And I did.

EIGHT

Frank Who?

I skipped school the next day. Took the subway back down to the vet's. Everybody who worked there knew I was a friend of Frank's. So this older woman from behind the desk let me come in the back and see Toto.

I don't think they do that for just everybody.

A couple of women passed us in the hall, and smiled at me like they felt sorry for me. Like they wished we could have better news.

She took me into a room full of cages. The dogs were all on one side, and two of them stood up and wagged their tails at me. One pawed gently at the bars. I guess we all just want to go home.

Toto was in a cage at about eye level. Flat out on his side. I'd never seen him looking relaxed. Well, I mean . . . I guess he was more than relaxed. He was unconscious. But it was still the only time I'd seen him not looking scared.

He had an IV dripping into his front leg. Taped to a patch of shaved skin.

"He's still trying to sleep off the anesthesia," she said.

"The swelling is better already."

"Well, yes. But that's easy. That's the main infection site. That'll start to drain right away. Now that the bad tooth is out."

"He looks so sweet when he's out like that." By the end of the sentence, I could feel my lip quivering like it was all I could do not to cry.

"Well . . . maybe he really *is* sweet. Under there somewhere."

"So, what now?"

"He's on some really powerful antibiotics. So we just have to wait and see if he responds or not. See which is stronger. The infection, or the combination of the antibiotics and his own immune system. The next forty-eight hours are . . ."

I'm pretty sure she must've kept talking. But I didn't hear any more. I looked up and saw Frank standing over by the door.

He caught my eye, and then I looked down at the floor again.

I didn't want to look at him. Because I didn't want to do that thing. That obvious thing. Where you look at him in a whole new light. Use the new information to look at him and see something entirely different. I didn't care to try on any new views of Frank.

"How's he doing?" Frank asked.

I just shrugged.

"Still a little touch and go," the woman said. "But he's still with us. He's a fighter."

My face felt hot, and I hated knowing I was probably blushing in front of both of them.

I was trying to think of the fastest way to get out of there when the woman said, "I'll be up front if you need anything." And bustled out.

I looked at Frank and he looked at me. Just for a second. I

could feel something heavy between us, like a metal partition. Something you can't see or hear through. Even Superman's X-ray vision would've been no match for it.

It was a lot like the energy two people tend to have when they like each other but they've been fighting. But Frank and I hadn't had a fight. He'd been nothing but kind to me.

He came over and stood beside me and looked into the cage with me. "I liked him better feisty," he said.

"Me too."

"You doing okay?"

"With what exactly?"

I would have bet you money I wasn't going to say anything like that. That I wasn't going to refer to that other matter in any way. I'm not sure what happened. It's like a capped volcano. Or a tube of toothpaste someone has been leaning on. Give it the slightest opening, you'll find out it's just waiting to spill.

"Take your pick," he said.

"I'm fine."

I said it the way people say they're fine when they're obviously not.

He put one hand on my shoulder. I ducked out from under it. It's not something I really thought out in advance. It just happened.

"I'm just upset about my cat," I said. "I'll call later and see how he's doing."

"Want me to call you on your cell if anything changes?"

"No thanks. I'll just call later."

I just wanted to go somewhere else. Anywhere else. Somewhere where I'm not always about to lose something. And maybe even where everyone is just about what you thought they were.

Wherever the hell that is.

I didn't look back on my way out. I wasn't anxious to see the look on his face. So I just walked away.

I went home, but it seemed weird and pointless to be there. There was nothing I wanted to do. I felt like I needed to throw myself into something. But identifying the something was proving tricky.

I felt like it would be a good time to have a friend. I could tell my friend all about my cat, and how worried and stressed out I was. And if it was a really good friend, I might even be able to talk about the thing with Frank. But that would have to be a pretty damn good friend. I didn't have anybody who was even close to that category.

I looked down at the leather bracelet on my wrist—I'd been wearing it pretty much every day—and I did think briefly about Wilbur. Maybe I could tell Wilbur about my cat. But I didn't even know Wilbur well enough to know if he liked cats. If he would understand.

I ate some crackers and then decided that my camera was my only real friend. I loaded up all my lenses and a couple extra rolls of film and took it all out to the street in search of Crazy Harry. I decided I would do a sort of photo essay on Crazy Harry. Maybe someone would look at the pictures and see what was so desperately lacking in his life. Maybe I could photograph the hole in Crazy Harry and it would mean something.

I'm not sure why I thought that. Except that something in my life had to mean something.

I sat on the stoop in front of our building for almost two hours. Until the sun moved across the sky so that I wasn't in the cool shade anymore, and then it got too hot to hang out and wait.

I never saw Crazy Harry. Maybe he was back on his meds and I'd missed my shot. Or maybe even crazy people need to take a day off now and then. One way or another, he never showed.

First, it made me mad. Here I'd lost all my friends except my camera, and I couldn't even get a break on something to shoot.

Then I decided it wasn't reasonable to assume that some perfect shot was going to be sitting there waiting for me just because I needed one.

I hated moods like that, where you feel like you need something to fill this big hole in you, and it has to be now. The hole never gets filled, somehow. The something is always just out of reach.

But then I thought, Maybe you can't just expect the shot to be there. Maybe you have to find it. Pursue it.

Maybe even create it.

I actually did go to school later that day. Briefly. But it wasn't so much about attending classes. Which I was still too upset to do. I don't think I would have been able to pay attention anyway, so it seemed pointless.

I actually went to find Wilbur.

And I did find him. After about twenty minutes of looking. Sitting cross-legged in a corner of one of the stairwell landings, reading a dog-eared paperback.

He looked up and smiled.

"Hey," I said. And sat down next to him.

"Hey."

"Where are you supposed to be?"

"Gym class. It's unbearable."

"Oh."

"Where are you supposed to be?"

"Home, I guess. Since I'm skipping school today. And I'll probably have to say I'm sick."

He put down the novel. "So if you're skipping school, isn't showing up here a little counterproductive?"

"Yeah, yeah, I know. But I wanted to ask you something."

I was hoping he wouldn't ask why I'd come all the way down to school to do it. Rather than just ask next time I saw him. Because it would have been tricky to explain. Part of that whole needing-something-right-now thing.

"Okay."

Now that I thought about it, Wilbur didn't ask a lot of questions.

"I wanted to know how you would feel about me taking pictures of you."

He glanced at the camera hanging around my neck. I'd brought it along in the hopes that we could do something immediate.

"For what?"

"I don't know. Just for me, I guess. I'm trying to learn photography. I just need a subject who's . . . you know . . . interesting."

"Interesting as in weird?"

"No. Not at all. Interesting. As in, somebody who looks like they have a story to tell."

He seemed to like that. I could see the difference on his face.

"Okay. I'll try it. So long as I get to see the pictures before you do anything with them. And you have to let me really be me. Which is a little more extreme than the way I come to school. And I'll have to get dressed and made up at your place. I can't leave home looking like that."

While he talked, I was having to let go of the idea of getting what I wanted on the spot. It hurt to feel it pulled away.

"When, then?"

"Maybe Saturday."

"Okay. I guess Saturday would be okay."

Which still left me with today to fill. But that really wasn't Wilbur's problem.

We sat there awhile longer in the corner of the landing, and he didn't pick up the book again. There was a beam of sunlight slanting down from a high window over our heads, and I watched bits of illuminated dust swirl in it.

"Do you like cats?" I asked after a time.

"I love cats. I used to have a cat. But my stepfather gave her away."

"Oh. I'm sorry."

My problems didn't seem so big compared to that. So I wasn't sure whether to say more or not.

"Why do you ask?"

"Oh. I guess I just wanted to talk to somebody because my cat is sick."

"Is he gonna be okay?"

"Not sure yet."

"I'm sorry."

We sat awhile longer. I watched dust swirl. Thinking it was probably always swirling like that. Everywhere. I just didn't usually see it so clearly.

Then Wilbur said, "If there's anything I can do . . ."

I was able to think of something immediately.

*   *   *

Wilbur and I walked all the way to the vet's office after school. I thought it would be better to walk. Like it would calm me down and tire me out and make it easier to be there.

Or maybe I just wanted to get there as slowly as possible.

I purposely didn't call ahead because I was scared of what they'd tell me. My gut felt like there must be bad news, and it would be better if I didn't know.

The woman with the wildly curly hair—who I'm pretty sure was a vet—was standing behind the counter with the receptionist when we came in. They were looking closely at a prescription bottle together. She looked up as I came through the door.

"Hey, you," she said. Kind of brightly. "Guess whose cat just sat up and drank some water?"

Even if she hadn't said anything at all, I knew just from the look on her face that I could stop bracing for the worst. I felt myself breathe—really breathe—for what felt like the first time in ages.

She said, "That's one strong cat you've got there."

I could feel myself smiling too widely.

I said, "Yeah. He's probably just too stubborn and ornery to die."

I got to bring Toto home a few days later. Friday. But there was a catch. He needed antibiotics twice a day. And I wasn't sure I could handle giving that cat a pill.

Of course Frank volunteered to help.

Which was very nice of him. Obviously. And it was just that sort of niceness that I'd always liked in Frank. And the least I could do was be grateful. And I was. In one very real way, I was.

But I had mixed feelings about having him knock on my door twice a day. And I felt like eighteen different kinds of garbage for not wanting to see him.

It's not that I didn't appreciate his help. And it's not like I was judging him for his life choices. It's more like . . . If I could just have more time to swallow things. Or maybe have things hit me in smaller pieces. I felt like life was always pushing too much down my throat too fast.

It was giving me serious indigestion.

He showed up for the first pill on Saturday morning. Not long before Wilbur was supposed to come over to get dressed and made up for our big photo shoot. He looked and sounded perkier than I felt.

"Pill time," he said.

"Thanks." I had Toto's antibiotics in my hand. "I'm sorry you have to do this."

"I don't mind. I told you I didn't mind."

But *I* sort of minded. Having to do this twice a day. And unfortunately, we'd both heard that. In the way I'd said it.

Toto was hiding in a cardboard box in a big kennel cage. Frank and I had set it up that way, so we could always catch him to give him his pill. Frank had carried the big collapsible cage home from work on the subway. I'd put a soft towel in a cardboard carton and stuck the box in there on its side. It didn't seem fair to not even give him someplace to hide. It was important to him, to hide.

I opened the cage and reached in and pulled the box out, and Frank got hold of the scruff of his neck. Then I held him down in the box by his shoulders and Frank gently opened his mouth and put the pill way back in his throat. Then we just sat there with him for a minute, with Frank holding his mouth closed and stroking his throat downward until he swallowed.

Toto was a stubborn cat. It took him a long time to swallow.

Frank said, "We're going to get past this, right?"

I felt a little stunned. I hadn't known we were going to talk about "it."

"Yeah. Of course."

"Because I don't want to see our friendship go anywhere."

"Me neither," I said.

And I meant it. I really felt it when I said it. Like I was just in a place of remembering how good it felt to be friends with Frank. And like all that other stuff was gone. But I knew better than to think it would stay gone forever. Or even much longer.

"If you ever have questions about—"

"No," I said. Too fast and too loud. Cutting him off too rudely. I didn't want to go into anything detailed. "No, it's not about having questions. It's not about not accepting you. It's . . ."

Yeah. Good one, Elle. Finish that sentence.

"I know what it is," he said.

Which had to be the most deeply uncomfortable and embarrassing thing anybody had ever said to me. Ever.

Thank God Toto finally swallowed.

"I'll come back this afternoon," Frank said.

I was so completely mortified that I didn't even walk him to the door. I didn't even say goodbye.

I've thought about that a lot since. That simple sentence. I'll come back this afternoon.

Nothing special about that. Right? No reason to doubt him. People say things like that all the time. You never question it. At the time, it never occurs to you that they could be flat-out wrong.

NINE

Right?

I walked out of my building with Wilbur, on our way to the park.

He was wearing a tight fishnet top with white pants. You could see his whole chest and shoulders right through the shirt. He was slim but kind of fit-looking, too. And his skin was dark.

Maybe Wilbur was Latino. Or part, anyway. I'd never really thought about it.

He was fully made up, but not in an extreme style. I mean, on a woman it wouldn't have been extreme. There was nothing exaggerated about it. The long top part of his hair had been pulled back into a tiny short pouf of a ponytail, which made the rest of his hair look sleek and flat. It was a more dramatic look, like when a woman skins her hair back to go formal.

I knew that a big part of my challenge would be to take photos that were about something bigger and more important. Just shooting the fact that Wilbur was feminine for a boy wouldn't be good enough. I had to go underneath that. Find something deeper and more to the point.

I just had no idea how.

About a dozen times in the past few days, I'd been tempted to go over and talk to Molly about it. But I kept getting hung up in the idea that Frank might be home. So I guess I was on my own with this. I'd have to figure it out from scratch.

Maybe everybody had to.

Maybe it's one of those things that can't really be taught in words, anyway.

We walked down East Drive to around Sixty-seventh Street before ducking into the park near Willowdell Arch. It was already really hot, so we sat in the shade of the dog statue. I was trying to think how you even start a project like this.

"Any idea why there's a statue of a dog over our heads?" I asked Wilbur. Probably just to have something to say.

I'd seen the statue before. I'd just never bothered to go over and read the plaque and see what it was all about.

"Sure," he said. "That's Balto. That Siberian husky who saved all those people in Alaska by getting some kind of medicine through in the winter. You know. A dogsled sort of a thing. He was the lead dog. The musher swears the dog found his way through the storm all by himself."

I wondered how Wilbur knew all that, but I didn't ask.

"Wow," I said. "A dog hero." Silence. It was time to take pictures. But Wilbur would want me to tell him what he was supposed to do. And I had no idea. "Do you like dogs?"

"I'm a little bit afraid of them," he said. "I'd be afraid of a big

Siberian like that. My mother used to have a little Yorkie. Pepito. I liked Pepito."

"What happened to him?" I asked. I was hoping this had nothing to do with his stepfather.

"He died of old age. And after he died, she never got another dog because my stepfather hates them."

We sat in silence in the shade for a few more beats.

"What feels like it's missing in your life?" I asked.

It was a weird question. Out of nowhere and not even fully explained. Or at least it should have come off that way. But Wilbur picked it right up. As if he'd been answering questions like that one all his life.

"Maybe feeling like I'm safe," he said.

"Okay, stand here in the shadow of this dog," I said. "And I'll see if I can find a way to see that through my camera lens."

But I wasn't even sure how I'd know if I succeeded. That was the problem with a film camera. Until you developed your film, you never knew if you got what you wanted or not.

I had him lean against the base of the dog statue. I liked the way it gave the shots the background of a hero.

"I'm not sure what I'm supposed to do," he said.

I lowered my camera and looked him right in the eye. "God's honest truth? Neither am I." I breathed deeply and thought about Molly. "Just be as close to yourself as you can possibly bring yourself to be."

Then I looked at him through the viewfinder again, and he was smiling.

"What? What are you smiling at?"

"Nothing. Really. I'm just not sure anybody ever said that to me before."

* * *

Right around the time I was packing up my lenses, Wilbur said this to me:

"I thought you'd be happier now that the cat is okay."

I didn't answer right off.

It was pretty clear what he was saying. It was an opening to talk about what was bothering me.

If I wanted to.

I'd been hoping it wasn't obvious that something was bothering me. But to Wilbur I guess it was.

I wound a whole roll of film back into the cartridge and popped it out of the camera before I said anything.

"If I tell you something, who all are you going to tell?"

"I don't gossip," he said.

"Nobody *says* they gossip. People just pass on what they've heard and at the same time they continue to think of themselves as people who don't gossip."

"When's the last time you heard me talk about anyone?"

"Good point," I said.

Another long silence.

Was I really going to do this thing? It felt scary. Maybe even insane. Then again, a better question might be: Was I really *not* going to do it, ever? Hold this up all by myself forever? Not take one single human being into my confidence?

I took a deep breath.

"Turns out he is," I said.

Now, that's another one of those statements that's hardly self-explanatory. I fully expected him to say, first, Who? And, second, Is what?

But it was Wilbur. Wilbur said no such thing.

"I know," he said.

"You said you didn't know."

"I guess I meant more like I didn't feel the need to say what I thought. I figure what people are can just be their own business."

We started walking together. Back out onto East Drive.

I never answered.

So, he'd pretty much thought so, too. But I figured I shouldn't be mad at him. After all, he'd kept his mouth shut.

Maybe I shouldn't be mad at any of them.

After all, they were right.

"Why does it bother you so much?" he asked. "Is it because you have a crush on him?"

"Oh, God. Is it that obvious?"

"Not obvious, really. I just figured you did."

"Yeah. I guess that's why."

"Okay. Because you don't strike me as the type who would get all weirded out about a thing like that. I mean, you get along fine with me."

"Yeah," I said. "I do." He was even starting to feel like a friend. "Are you trans?"

"Not really. Not the way he is. I mean, I don't want to have surgery. I don't need to be a girl. I'm just this."

Then we walked without talking for a while.

"I won't tell anybody," he said.

"Thanks," I said.

I'm not the most trusting soul in the world. But I believed him.

We walked the rest of the way home together. Being with him as a friend was starting to feel more comfortable. It was the last time anything would feel comfortable for a very long time.

Just before we turned the corner onto my street, the shriek of an ambulance hit us, just out of nowhere, and very close. Not like it had come from far away, getting louder all the time. Like the ambulance had just pulled away from the curb and turned on its siren. Right around the corner.

Right on my block.

I winced as it streaked by us. Man. Those things are really ear-splitting up close.

We turned the corner and saw a crowd still gathered. Right in front of my building. That sort of aimless ending point in the gathering of a crowd, when there's no real reason for them to be gathered anymore, and they almost miss their reasons. Like they're waiting to stock up the energy to go back inside.

There was blood on the street.

"Somebody must have got hit by a car," I said to Wilbur. At least, I hoped it was something accidental like that. I guess somebody could've been shot, but my brain didn't want to go there.

"Do you know any of your neighbors?" he asked. Indicating the gathering of people.

Right up until he said that, I hadn't really looked at them as my neighbors. They were just a bunch of strangers to me. The only neighbors I knew were Frank and Molly. I scanned the crowd for them and came up empty.

"Nope. Not a one."

I waited nervously in the doorway of my building while

Wilbur talked to two very old women. I was wondering how he had the nerve to do that.

He nodded about four times, then walked to where I was waiting. Or hiding, as the case may have been.

"Something about Crazy Harry," he said. "He came up behind some guy and started yelling. Startled him right out into the street, and the guy got hit by a cab."

"Jesus," I said. Then I wondered if Wilbur was a Christian. I thought I'd seen him wear a little gold cross once. Maybe I'd said something offensive. "Did they say who it was?"

Which was something of a stupid question, of course. I didn't know any of my neighbors. So why would one name be different from any other?

"They didn't know. They just said a young man. Which, you know . . . to them . . ." He looked over his shoulder at them. They were still gathered. Looking down at the blood and shaking their heads. "Could be fifty."

"Oh. Well . . ." It felt weird to say goodbye to Wilbur and be alone. But I wasn't sure why. Definitely something about the blood on the street in front of my building. Someone could have been killed for all I knew. "Thanks for walking me home."

"You okay?"

"Oh, yeah," I said. "I'm fine."

Part of me hoped he would hear the lie in that, and stay. But it was Wilbur. Wilbur takes people at their word.

It took me about five minutes to decide to knock on Frank and Molly's door. Or, at least, to get up the nerve to do what I'd decided.

I mean, one of our neighbors had been hit by a car right outside our front stoop. If I couldn't put my issues aside at a time like that, what would it say about me?

Maybe they would know who the poor guy was. And if he was going to be okay.

Maybe Frank would want to play Scrabble. Just like the old days.

Maybe Molly would cut up some organic fruit and feed us.

Maybe George and Gracie would rub up against my legs and purr.

Maybe then I wouldn't have to feel like this.

I knocked. I waited. I waited some more. I knocked again. I waited even longer.

I was stunned by the depth of my own disappointment. Turned out I had needed them to be home. Badly. And I hadn't even known it.

Until they weren't.

It seemed funny that they weren't home on a Saturday. Frank's day off. Usually he's tired and really happy to just take a nap on the couch on Saturday. But I guess there are a million places that people can be.

I gave up standing in front of their door, but it was hard. I went back inside my own apartment. Climbed outside on my fire escape. Sat looking down at the blood.

The crowd had dispersed.

Funny, but the cars were all going around that spot. The blood was still fresh-looking and red, and they had just taken down the police tape, but the street hadn't been hosed off yet and nobody wanted to drive through it. I guess it was just a normal human reaction to a thing. Even if they had to stop and wait for a spot to open up so they could drive around it. It was like the wrong end of a magnet, only redder.

Near one side of the red patch, I saw something. Something I hadn't seen from the street. Maybe somebody's feet had been blocking it.

Maybe I just hadn't wanted to look too close.

From my fire-escape perch, it looked like a pair of glasses.

At first, it didn't hit me. Then it did.

I ran straight down the fire-escape stairs to the street. Telling myself lots of people wear glasses. Maybe one person in every three or four. Right? Well, who knows what the statistics are? Who cares? But lots.

It didn't mean a thing.

Right?

The ladder wouldn't go down. It was all rusty and old. So I jumped. Landing on the sidewalk hurt like hell, mostly in my shins and on the bottom of my feet. But I didn't stop to pay attention to any of that.

I stepped out into the street and looked down at the glasses. I remember my insides going numb, but not much else about how I felt. You know what? You want the truth? I didn't. I didn't feel. At all.

I reached down and picked up the round wire-rimmed glasses. Frank's glasses.

One lens was broken. But I picked them up just the same. At the time I reached for them, I wasn't focused on the fact that they had been lying in the blood. But then a drop of it fell, hit the street near my foot, and splashed onto one of my favorite old lace-up boots.

In slow motion.

That's how I knew I felt something in the middle of all that nothing. Because that drop took forever to hit the street. I felt like I could recite the Gettysburg Address while I was watching it fall.

Weird thing is, I had no idea why I picked up the glasses. Maybe I thought Frank would want them back again. Broken lens and all. Because there would definitely still be a Frank to want his glasses back.

Right?

TEN

Clothes. And Control.

I have no idea how long I sat in that position. My back against Frank and Molly's door. The broken glasses hanging from my left hand. My head leaned back. Staring at a scuff on the wallpaper, right across from me.

It's possible I might even have dozed off briefly. Because it definitely got late while I was sitting there.

I would tell the truth about what I was thinking if I remembered. And if I were sure I was thinking.

It was late when I heard them come up the stairs. Somehow I knew it was them, even before they came up onto the landing. I knew this was what I was waiting for. My head said it could be any neighbor who lived on this floor. But this little spot under my sore stomach said, No. This is it.

When they came into view, it was Frank, alive and on his feet. But barely. On one side of him was Molly. On the other side, a woman who looked about fifty, with long, thick white hair. Somebody I had never met.

I tried to jump up, but my muscles didn't move. I tried to say something, but nothing got said.

Frank's head was shaved right down to the skin. All over. He had a big patch of bandage taped to one side of it. And his right arm had been splinted and wrapped in a sling, which looked like it made him hard to grip on Molly's side. She had to wrap her arms around his waist to hold him up.

Just for a split second, I might've thought, Why did they let him out of the hospital in that condition? But, if so, the thought scooted right away again.

By now, I was looking straight up at them as they stood over me. Molly was digging around in her purse, probably looking for her keys.

I think Frank looked at me. It was hard to tell how alert he was. How much he was actually taking in. But his eyes roamed across the doorway and landed on my face and paused there. And just in that moment, the things I hadn't dared think came up and got thought all at once. Fell all over each other and tangled up in the thinking.

If he had died . . .

It's one thing to lose your best friend. It's another thing entirely to lose your best friend while you're treating him like shit. Before you even have a chance to make it up to him.

Guilt. I felt it. Big. Had it been there all along? I had no idea.

"Thank God," I said out loud. "Thank God he's okay."

"He's not that okay," Molly said. Her voice sounded tight. It sounded like her voice but with somebody else's disposition in charge of the tone. She had her keys in her hand now. "You want to move, hon? We need to get him inside."

I scrambled away from the door so fast that I tripped and ended up on my hands and knees on the hall carpet. My knee landed on the broken glasses, breaking them further. I left them where I squashed them. When I made it to my feet again, they were helping Frank through the door.

I followed them in.

I hadn't exactly been invited. I definitely hadn't asked permission. Probably because I wasn't sure I'd get it.

I just needed to go in. I needed to be there with them. With him. I needed to be a part of this. So I didn't ask. I took advantage of their one-pointed focus.

Nobody told me to go home.

For the first hour or so, I sat in the living room by myself. The lights were off everywhere but in the bedroom. I sat on the floor by the window, as if I'd take up less space there. As if no one would notice. No one to catch me feeling guilty.

I rested my chin on the windowsill and watched the empty street. It seemed strange that the street should be so empty, even in the middle of the night. It was Saturday night. Where was everybody?

Not even Crazy Harry.

But there was a good reason for that. They had taken him away. Thank God.

I pictured him pacing under a streetlight. Marching back and forth under that circle of light, shaking his head back and forth. As if arguing with someone who wasn't even there. Or maybe with himself. The way he would have been. If everything were normal.

I heard a little noise, and looked up to see Molly standing near me, looking out the window. Close enough that I could have reached out and touched her. Of course, I didn't.

"Somebody should do something about him," I said.

"Who, Harry?"

"Yes. Harry."

"They did. They took him into custody."

"I hope they never let him out."

"They have to let him out. When he's back on his meds, he'll come home."

"They shouldn't let him come back here. He shouldn't be allowed to live here."

"Then where should he be allowed to live?" she asked.

A moment later, when it was clear to both of us that I wasn't going to answer, she said, "I'm going to make tea. Would you like a cup of tea?"

"Yes, please," I said.

Like a five-year-old.

I felt like an obstacle in the lives of everyone who came near me. I felt like the stupidest, most abhorrent person in the galaxy. I shouldn't even be allowed to live around decent people.

Then again, I guess I have to live somewhere. Don't I?

"How bad is it?" I asked.

We were sitting around the kitchen table. Me, Molly, and Liz. That other woman's name was Liz. She was a nurse. And their friend.

We had been drinking tea for a long time before I got up the nerve to ask.

Molly sighed, as though she just didn't have the energy to

answer. She tossed her eyes over to Liz, who spoke for her. Like they did their thinking with only one mind between the two of them.

"His right wrist is shattered," she said. "Complex series of breaks in his elbow. He'll need orthopedic surgery. And tons of physical therapy. That's not really the biggest problem, though. Not right now. Right now the head injury is the worry. They can be dangerous. Tricky."

"Why did they even release him from the hospital, then?"

A silence as Molly and Liz exchanged looks.

For a while, I thought nobody was ever going to answer me. Such a simple question, too.

"They didn't," Molly said. "He left against medical advice. They wanted to admit him. But he refused."

"*Why?*"

No answer. Just silence.

"That's crazy. Why would he do that?" I could hear my voice come up. I was disturbed by the tone and volume of my own spoken thoughts.

"He had a bad experience in a hospital."

"So? I have bad experiences in school all the time, but I still go."

Molly pushed back from the table suddenly. The squeal of her chair legs on the linoleum startled me. A splash of hot tea sloshed out of the cup and onto my hand. I didn't say ouch, though it would have been easy.

"I'm too tired to explain it to her," Molly said. I guess she was talking to Liz. She sounded exasperated. Like I was getting on her last nerve.

She stomped out of the room.

112

I heard the bedroom door close.

I looked up at Liz, but she was looking down at the table.

"Is Molly mad at me?"

"I guess you'd have to ask Molly about that," she said.

A long silence, during which I took a paper napkin from the holder in the middle of the table and used it to mop up my spilled tea.

"Other than outright hate crimes"—Liz's voice startled me—"the two most terrifying experiences for someone in transition are hospitals and jails." That sat on the table for a moment. I wasn't quite sure what I was supposed to do with it. "Think about it. Put yourself in his position. In the hospital, they take away the two most important things in the world for somebody like Frank. Your clothes. And your control. All it takes is one bigot. One sadist. He had a really bad experience back when they lived in South Carolina."

South Carolina? Molly and Frank lived in South Carolina? I had no idea. How could I not know that about them?

"Yeah, but . . . South Carolina. That's like a different world. This is New York. It wouldn't happen here."

"You sure? You want to guarantee him it couldn't happen? Like I said. It only takes one."

I had no idea what to say. My thoughts tangled around for a few minutes, and then arrived at the simplest possible statement.

"Could he die?"

"Not if I have anything to say about it. I'll monitor his condition all night. If I think there's any bleeding or swelling on his brain, we'll get him back to the emergency room, pronto."

"But . . . if he could die . . . How can he not go to the hospital if he could die?"

She didn't answer for a long time. Just sipped at her tea. I thought maybe it was a question with no answer.

Then she said, "Maybe he'd rather die with his dignity intact."

I heard myself make a funny sound. A muffled noise. I think I started out to say Oh, God, but it ended up coming out as a grunt. It made me sick to think about that. So I closed my eyes and said nothing at all. And, as much as possible, thought nothing at all.

"I've got his back," Liz said. "Which is better than nothing."

I woke up on my back on the couch, with Gracie sleeping on my chest. It was hard to breathe all the way in, but I liked the warm weight of her, and she looked comfortable, so I didn't ask her to move.

From the corner of my eye, I saw Molly sitting in a hard-back chair by the window. As if she was waiting for something. I wondered what she was waiting for.

I scratched Gracie behind the ears for a minute, and then it hit me.

"Oh shit!" I saw Molly jump. "I forgot Toto. I didn't give him his afternoon pill."

"You better go home and take care of your cat," she said. Her voice sounded cool.

I eased Gracie off my chest and onto the couch. "If I do, can I still come back?"

"Maybe you should just stay with Toto and get some rest."

I stood up. Humiliatingly, I had to fight to keep tears back. "Did I do something to make you mad?"

I thought it was brave to just spit it right out like that.

She sighed. Still looking out the window. Not at me. She didn't answer.

"Are you just scared and worried about Frank, or are you really mad at me?"

"A little of both, I guess."

I stood taking that in. Feeling a little woozy. Unsteady on my feet. Maybe because I had just wakened up. Maybe because I'd only had forty-five minutes of sleep all night. Maybe because of Frank lying in the other room, his brain about to bleed and swell.

Maybe because of Molly's last sentence. Which, by the way, was a walk in the park compared to her next sentence.

"Don't you think Frank has feelings?"

My mouth felt numb while I tried to answer. "Yeah. Of course he does."

"He likes you so much. He really cares about you. How do you think it makes him feel when you treat him like he has an infectious disease? Don't you think that hurts him?"

I lost my battle with the tears. They ran down my face. Dropped onto my shirt. I even watched one hit my boot. The same boot. That boot had seen a lot of life in the past few hours.

"I'm sorry," I said.

Then I slunk back to my own apartment.

The phone blasted me out of sleep. I opened my eyes, then winced them closed again. It was light. Too light.

Another ring.

I grabbed it up. It was Liz.

"Oh, thank God you're there," she said. "We have to get

Frank back to the hospital. Molly and I are going to bring him down the stairs. If you want to help, go down and get us a cab, okay?"

The line went dead.

I'd been sleeping on top of the covers with all my clothes on. So I just got up and ran. Grabbed my key off the table on the way out the door.

I took the stairs two at a time, even though I felt like I was doing it in my sleep. Like I was dreaming about running down the stairs.

But I had been asked to do something to help. And I was going to do it right. I was going to do such a good job on it that Frank would be okay. I was going to do my one little part so perfectly that Molly would forgive me. The pain I'd caused Frank would be drowned out and erased by the perfection of my ability to get a cab when one was needed.

I blasted out into the barely cool morning. Into the street.

I saw a cab coming immediately and raised my hands. Waved frantically. Jumped up and down like a fool.

He saw me. He was going to stop. He pulled up to where I stood.

Perfect. Perfect. Perfect.

I opened the back door of the cab.

A man with a black trench coat and a briefcase jumped in.

At first, I just stood there with my mouth open. I did not let go of the door.

"Thanks, hon," he said. "I'm in a hurry."

"Get out of my cab."

"I flagged him first. You just didn't see me."

I held the door more tightly. Leaned in. I caught the driver's eyes in the rearview mirror.

"Did you stop for him or for me?"

"I stop for you," he said. He had some kind of African-sounding accent. Lilting.

"Get out of my cab," I said to the briefcase guy.

"It's really an emergency, hon."

I almost screamed. I opened my mouth to scream. I was going to let him know what a real emergency looked like. For a second, I thought I might literally grab hold of him and drag him out onto the street. Or try, anyway.

But I didn't. I was right at the edge of violence. But I didn't commit any.

I left the door open. And I made my way to the front of the cab really fast. And I sat on the hood. Right on the driver's side. Right in his view. Right where he wouldn't be able to see the road if he drove away. Which was a moot point, of course, anyway. Because he wasn't going to drive away.

Not now.

I felt the heat of the hood through my jeans, and the vibration of the engine. This steady thrumming under my butt.

A moment later, I turned around to see Molly and Liz helping Frank into the cab. They were really carrying more than helping. He seemed completely unconscious.

I watched them struggle to get him into the backseat. Which, by the way, was empty. I looked around and saw Briefcase Guy walking in the street, inside the row of parked cars, looking for another cab.

I jumped off the hood and into the front seat, next to the

driver. Before anybody could tell me not to. Before they could leave without me.

We had pulled away from the curb and driven two blocks before I consciously realized I was still in my sock feet.

Liz's voice. "Have you lived in New York all your life?"

No answer. I thought she was talking to the cabdriver. Though, truthfully, it seemed like a funny time to be making small talk.

It took me a minute to realize she might have been asking me. "Who? Me?"

"Yes, you."

"Yeah, I was born here. Why?"

"Remind me never to try to steal a cab from you," she said.

ELEVEN

A Special Kind of Idiot

It was almost eight o'clock that evening when Molly found me in the hospital lobby.

I had been trying to stay out of the way without actually going home.

It's not like I could really be with Frank anyway. First, he was in the OR for this procedure—which I had been working really hard not to visualize—where they drill a tiny hole in his skull and insert a drain. Then after that, he was in a recovery room.

I think about an hour earlier they'd put him in a regular room, and I think Molly and Liz got to sit in there with him. But I couldn't bring myself to push my way into that scene. I felt like it was their moment, not mine.

I felt like I didn't deserve it.

I was wrong to think that acing getting a cab would fix everything. It didn't.

I instinctively jumped up when I saw her.

"Is he okay? Is everything okay?"

"It went well," she said. Long pause. The energy surrounding the pause didn't quite fit the atmosphere of good news. "But he definitely has to stay the night. At least one night. If we're really lucky."

"What did Frank have to say about that?"

"Nothing. He's still unconscious."

I sat down hard. I'm not sure how long I was staring at that weird pattern of linoleum floor—and my own ridiculous sock feet—before Molly sat down beside me.

"Poor Frank," I said. "What if he wakes up in the night? He'll be so scared."

No answer. After a time, I looked over at Molly, and I could see she'd been crying. Why hadn't I seen that before? Why hadn't I looked closer?

"Maybe they'd let you stay with him?"

A snort of laughter. "We've been through it with them, Elle. For almost an hour. Bottom line, Frank and I can't get legally married at this point, and I can't stay past visiting hours if I'm not a spouse. I know it's not fair and you know it's not fair, but they obviously feel it's not their problem. I have no legal connection to Frank. Like it or not. I tried reasoning with them. I tried shouting. Cajoling. Threatening. All it got me was the promise of a call to hospital security."

A long pause. That linoleum pattern was so weird. Black and white. It burned itself onto my eyes so that when I squeezed them shut, I could still literally see the pattern on the insides of my eyelids. And I'd been staring at it for most of the day. But I only just thought about it now.

"You could sneak in," I said.

Another bitter snort of laughter. "After the stink I made? They would never take their eyes off me."

Another moment of silence. During which I knew something. Something that was important. That was real. It just took me a moment to form it into words and say it out loud.

"I didn't make a stink. They don't even know I'm connected to Frank."

I looked over at Molly, but her face didn't show much. Just wear.

After a minute, she said, "It's possible that you could get arrested."

"So?"

"Besides. What would you do? I mean, even if somebody did give him a hard time . . . what could you do about it?"

"She would sit on the jerk's hood." Liz's voice, just out of nowhere.

It startled us both. I jumped, and I felt Molly jump beside me.

"Come on, Molly," Liz said. "I'm taking you home. You need sleep."

Molly rose heavily to her feet, and both women stood over me for a minute. I looked up into Molly's face.

She said, "Liz, could you please get a cab? I'll be right out."

Unfortunately, I knew what that meant. Big talk. I braced for the worst. Like a fighter tightening up his ab muscles just before the gut shot.

"I owe you an apology," Molly said.

I blinked. Too much, I think. I felt my gut untie its knots. "You do?"

"I feel I do, yes."

"Why?"

"I shouldn't have lost my temper with you. You know. Before. I don't know if you can understand this. But Frank is so helpless right now. And I'm trying so hard to defend him. It's like anybody who's ever hurt him—anybody who's ever even thought about hurting him—better watch out. But it wasn't fair of me to take it out on you. I'm sorry."

"You don't have to be sorry." Long silence. I had no idea what else to say. And I was refusing to look at her face. At last, I thought of something that felt safe. "If I give you my key," I said, fishing around in my pocket for it, "will you give Toto his pill tonight and in the morning? He missed another two today. I'm starting to get scared that he won't get better. You know. If I keep skipping his pills."

I held the key out to her. On the flat of my palm. I expected her to just take it. But instead, she took the whole hand. Held it a minute, and squeezed it.

"Frank's in two twenty-three," she said.

Then she let go. I looked at my palm and the key was gone.

When I looked up, so was she.

I had about half a dozen stealthy plans for how to do this. But it was all too easy.

I was almost disappointed.

When I got to Frank's floor, there was still a good ten minutes of visiting hours left. So I just walked in. No one said a word to me, or even looked at me. I walked by a nurses' station staffed by three female nurses—one of whom had probably threatened to call security on Molly—but none of them even looked up.

Frank lay unconscious in a double room. Thank God that

drain thing was covered completely in bandages. His whole head was covered in bandages. He looked small and frail. Younger than he usually looked to me. I'm not a motherly type, but he almost brought that out in me now.

In the next bed lay a strong candidate for oldest woman on the planet. She must have been a hundred and something. Her hair was just a faded wisp, barely covering her scalp, allowing a mass of dark age spots to show through. She looked at least unconscious. If not dead.

I had to swallow my irritation over the fact that they put Frank in a room with a woman roommate. I was beginning to see more of the point about the whole hospital and jail experience.

It wasn't hard to find a place to hide. Not an absolutely perfect place, but the best I had available to me. It would do. It would have to.

The white curtain that divided the area between the beds extended most of the way around the head of Frank's bed. Not all the way down to the floor. That would have been nice. But the gap wasn't really all that huge.

I slipped into the bathroom and found a ridiculously white bleached towel. And then I disappeared. I slid under Frank's bed, tucked myself behind the curtain, then used the towel to cover the parts of me that weren't white. If I hadn't been under the bed, it might have been pretty obvious. But to see me, somebody would have to pull the curtain all the way back on one side of the bed or the other and then look under the bed. And even then, once the lights went out, I'd be hard to spot.

I wondered when that would be.

And if it didn't work? Well, then they could arrest me.

It was too cramped under the bed to sit up normally. I curled up as best I could. And waited. For what, I wasn't sure.

It was dawning on me, I think, that it was going to be a long night.

I woke out of a sound sleep, hurting. My back hurt from sleeping at that weird angle. One hip bone hurt from the hard floor. My muscles felt locked into place.

But it was dark. And completely silent. I had no idea what time it was. But it was late. Night shift. And I had not been busted.

Yet.

I came out of hiding.

The oldest woman in the world was snoring. More loudly than I ever imagined it was possible for a real person to snore in real life. I thought only cartoon characters and old men in fifties sitcoms sounded like that.

On the plus side, it meant she was alive.

For about an hour, I sat in the chair next to Frank's bed. In the dark. My eyes were pretty well adjusted to the lack of light, so I could just about make out the contours of his face.

I know this next bit will sound weird. But here's what I was thinking:

Two things.

One. We would never treat anybody like shit if we knew they could be about to die. I mean, anyone we care about even a little. If we knew they could die, we would just freaking get over all the petty crap, because losing someone you love is more important than any of that. But, now, here's the part that actually took up some of the hour: Anybody could be about to die. Every single person we care about is going to die. And we have no idea when.

So how can we afford to treat anybody like shit? Well, that's the easy part. We can't. But here's the harder part: Since we all know for a fact that we're all going to die, why don't we all treat each other like we could lose each other at any minute? Because we all know it's true.

That was actually the good part of my thinking. The happy stuff, in comparison.

Now. At the distinct risk of sounding weirder still:

Two. You feel something for somebody. And then you find out they're not what you thought they were. So the feelings go away, right? Because, you know, they were based on something that's gone now. Right? Wrong. I kept looking at Frank, wanting those feelings to be gone. They were not gone. What if they never would be?

I heard a sudden noise, and jumped a mile. The door. Someone was opening the door to Frank's room. My first impulse was to dive back under the bed, but there wasn't time. I'd get caught out in the open. So I just hit the floor behind the chair. Just huddled in the corner, squatting there more or less in plain sight, with nothing but a plastic chair to block someone's view of me.

The good news, if there can be good news in a spot like this, is that the sudden visitor was a nurse—I assumed—working with a small beam of flashlight. If she turned on the lights, it would all be over. By flashlight, I just might get by.

I watched her checking on the ancient woman in the next bed. I don't know what she was checking, but it seemed to take forever. I was squatting in a position that was hard to hold for long. My calf muscles were getting trembly, and my sock feet wanted to slip on the shiny floor. I was worried I might topple right over.

In time, she moved around to Frank's bed. I saw white pant

legs just a foot or two in front of my face. I saw her shine the flashlight on the bandages on Frank's head and begin to gently peel back the outer layer.

I quick looked away.

By the time she was done checking Frank's drain and had the bandage back in place, I was so unsteady and so trembly that I was afraid my movements would catch her eye. I reached out to steady myself by holding the chair. It moved slightly, scraping on the linoleum.

The nurse looked up. Looked my way.

She turned on the little reading light by Frank's bed. Shined it in my direction. Just before I blinked into the light, I was surprised to see that she was not a she at all. It was a male nurse.

I plunked into a sit. Having nothing left to lose.

He walked over to where I was sitting and squatted in front of me.

My whole body turned to ice. Somehow, getting arrested didn't seem like such a small deal anymore.

"Well. Who do we have here?"

"Only me," I said. Hoping against hope that he had a sense of humor.

He was about in his late twenties, and handsome. One dark, curly mass of hair hung down between his eyebrows like the forelock on a horse. He had a Velcro-length beard and long, thick, dark eyelashes.

"What are you doing here, little one?"

"Taking care of my friend Frank."

"I thought that was my job."

"I'm watching his back."

"Against what?"

He waited a minute for me to answer, but I didn't know what to say. Maybe too much information would only hurt Frank's situation. So I said nothing at all.

"Oh wait. I know. You think maybe some vicious trans-phobic asshole is going to take advantage of him in his helpless state. Well, not on my watch, girlfriend. I'm the only one assigned to this floor tonight. And I'm family."

I think my mouth might have been hanging open.

"You're related to Frank?"

He threw back his head and overflowed with quiet laughter. It sounded so genuinely gleeful that it actually made me smile. Against odds. I think it was contagious.

"Not that kind of family, honey. The GLBT variety. The community."

It's not as if I'd never heard the expression before. More that my brain was moving in low gear.

Before I could answer, he said, "Gay . . ." A pause, as if he were teaching lessons to kindergartners. "Lesbian . . ."

"Right, bisexual, transgender. I know. Oh. I get it. You mean you're gay."

His index finger reached out and touched the tip of my nose. Pushed it slightly. "You're slow, baby girl, but at least you get there eventually. Nothing bad is gonna happen to your friend on my shift. Over my dead body."

"Thank God." For the first time since I heard the door opening, I breathed. Really breathed. "Can I stay with him anyway?"

I was still worried that he would wake up alone in this room, and the nice male nurse would be nowhere around, and Frank would be scared. I wasn't even here mostly because I was worried someone would hurt or humiliate him. Because the chances of that were fairly small. I was here so he wouldn't have to be afraid someone would.

"Well, you *have* to stay now. You're committed. You can't just go sauntering by security in the middle of the night. You're here till seven a.m., girlfriend. Like it or not."

"Thank you," I said. As he pulled to his feet. "For not busting me."

"Yeah, and just one thing about that. I could lose my job for letting you stay. If I knew you were here. So it's a good thing I never saw you, right?"

"Right! You never saw me."

"We never had this conversation."

"What conversation?"

He reached down and pushed the tip of my nose one more time.

He winked at me just before he turned out the light. Then he slipped out of the room.

After he left, I sat in the same chair, staring at the same Frank. But I could feel how the energy in the room had shifted. I wasn't afraid anymore. I wasn't hiding out. Or feeling like I was surrounded by enemies.

The night was different and so was I.

After a while I moved, and sat on the edge of Frank's bed, because I wanted to look at him more closely. I had to go around to the other side because I was afraid of bumping his poor right arm.

I reached out and touched his face, then took my hand back. Waited for a while to make sure I hadn't wakened him up. No movement. So I touched him again.

I ran my hand down his cheek and his chin. Over the stubble

of five o'clock shadow. He must have been taking hormones. Because it was definitely the right feel for a man's face. It reminded me, in a big strong flash, of my father. When I was really little. I haven't seen my father in a long time.

I ran my hand gently over the outside of his ear. It was small and perfectly shaped. Sculptured. Like a seashell.

Something was building up in my stomach, a sort of electricity. I felt as though I were stealing something. Cheating somehow. I'd never imagined what it would feel like to be with Frank while he was unconscious. I could sit with him, stare at him, touch him. All in secret.

Was I invading his privacy? I wasn't sure. But I think the little electric buzz in my stomach thought I was.

Why did I still feel the same way about him? How could it still be like that?

But a little voice in the back of my head—well, not exactly in the back of my head, more like in a spot *over* my head—said "why" and "how" questions were almost never helpful. Things either aren't or they are. All the wondering why in the world won't make things anything but just what they are.

I was sleepy, and tired of sitting up, so I lay down on the little piece of bed that Frank didn't fill. I was afraid of crushing his left arm, so I picked it up and tucked under it.

If the nurse came back, he'd think I was insane. But he probably wouldn't come back. Besides, maybe he wouldn't think that. Maybe he would just think I loved Frank. Maybe he already thought I was Frank's partner. That was a weird flash that came into my head. It felt strange, but also kind of good, to think we were an actual possibility in somebody's eyes.

I have no idea how long I lay beside him that way, his arm

draped over my shoulder. But I do know that I was right on the edge of sleep. That weird patch of no-man's-land when you're not fully asleep but dream images start invading your brain.

I said something, but I wasn't sure if I said it out loud. Maybe I just thought it. Maybe I just dreamed I said it out loud.

Anyway, here's what it was:

"I love you, Frank."

And then, when I heard it, either out loud or in my head, it startled me awake again. And I realized I was crying.

I sat up and reached for a tissue from the little table near the bed.

I felt a hand on my back. There was only one person it could possibly have belonged to.

"That's so sweet," Frank said. He sounded a little bit like he was talking in his sleep.

I jumped to my feet and took about three steps back from the bed, hearing his hand fall hard back onto the mattress.

"Oh my God. You aren't supposed to be awake. You weren't supposed to hear that."

No answer. His eyes were still closed. For a minute, I thought maybe he'd really been talking in his sleep. Literally.

Then he said, "Sorry."

"You're supposed to be unconscious," I said. I know. What an idiot. But that's what I said. "You're supposed to be all doped up on painkillers."

His eyes flickered open and then closed themselves again. "I do feel a little dopey," he said. His words running together.

It struck me that I was supposed to be thrilled that he was conscious and talking. And all I could think about is what I'd said. And how I shouldn't have said it. And how he shouldn't have heard it.

"Am I in the hospital?" he asked. Sounding a little sharper.

"Yes. I'm sorry. It couldn't be helped."

A long, long silence. I walked around to the far side of the bed again. Sat down on the hard plastic chair.

Then, after a time, he said, "What are you doing here?"

"Watching your back."

"That's very sweet."

"I'm such an idiot."

"Why?"

"*Why?* Why do you think? What kind of idiot says something like that to an unconscious person and then starts to cry?"

Another long pause. Literally a minute or two. As though he were napping between sentences.

"A sweet one?"

I sat up straight for a long time, waiting for him to say more. Terrified of what it might be. But after that, I think he went back down into his drugged sleep for real.

Sometime, just as it was getting light outside, I looked up to see the world's oldest woman awake and watching me in the faded light. It startled me a little. Snoring aside, I still thought of her as being in some loose category of the state of dead.

"Are you an angel?" she asked. Full-on serious. I swear.

"No," I said. "I'm not. Far from it."

"You look like an angel," she said.

"I don't feel like one."

She closed her eyes again. The corner of one side of her

mouth twitched up a tiny bit. Like she was wearing about 20 percent of a little smile.

Just a hair after seven o'clock, a female nurse appeared. Opened the door and left it that way. A little blond woman who I swear couldn't have stood any taller than four foot ten.

The shifts must have changed.

She looked at me strangely.

"It's too early for you to be in here," she said. Not harshly. Just sharing information. "Visiting hours don't start until eight."

"Really? Eight? I thought it was seven."

"Nope. Eight."

"Okay. Sorry. I'll wait out in the hall."

"There's a waiting room one floor down."

"No thanks," I said. "I'll wait in the hall. I'm watching my friend's back."

"What do you think is going to happen to . . ."

I could feel her fishing around for a finish to that sentence. And I knew what her problem was. Happen to *him*? Couldn't be. This was a room for female patients. To *her*? The heavy growth of beard made that tricky.

". . . this patient?"

"Kind of a long story," I said.

I scooted past her, hoping she wouldn't notice my lack of shoes. And I sat cross-legged in the hall, my back against the door-jamb of Frank's room.

For quite a long time.

"You're here early."

I looked up to see Molly standing over me. She gave me a

little wink to go with the words. A little signal that the sentence had only been playacting.

I looked away again. I couldn't bring myself to look into Molly's eyes. Or even at her face. I felt nervous and guilty. Uncomfortable. As if I had trespassed against her.

She didn't seem to notice.

"Toto is okay, as far as I can tell," she said. "I gave him his two pills. And I cleaned his litter box. He still has plenty of dry food but I gave him a can of wet in case his mouth still hurts. And I freshened up his water."

"Thank you," I said. Still not looking.

"Here. I brought you a present."

I looked up just as far as her outstretched hand. No farther. My big old lace-up boots.

"Thank you," I said. "Just what I've always wanted."

"I figured I owed you one."

"Not really," I said. Putting on my boots, right there in the hall, as an excuse to keep looking down. "The way I see it, we're only just barely even."

I walked all the way home. The morning was just recently fully light, the air motionless but cool. I had enough money in my pocket to take a bus or the subway, but I didn't.

It was Monday, I figured out with some effort. A school day. But I knew I wouldn't go.

I took a longcut through the park.

I wanted to be outside. I felt alive, more so than usual, and I wanted to hang on to the feeling.

I saw a woman in spandex walking four dogs—all boxers—on leashes, and I smiled at her, and she smiled back. I passed a small, very temporary homeless camp. Four men huddled on the pavement in a tight-knit circle. One of them looked up, and I was hit with a strange feeling that I was not so very apart from them. It came out of nowhere, and I didn't quite know what to make of it.

After that, I nursed the feeling. Looked for it everywhere. In the birds and the squirrels. In the bus exhaust and the traffic lights as I came back out onto the boulevard. Even in the cigarette smoke of people passing by. Some indefinable sense of being part of everything. Not really being separate from the rest of reality.

I purposely didn't think too much, but when I got to my building, I wondered again if Frank would forget my visit. And, most specifically, forget what I had said to him. It worried me, yet it seemed reasonable to expect he wouldn't remember.

Then again, that weird voice over my head said to me, Maybe it's just the truth. Maybe it doesn't require any forgetting.

TWELVE

Information, and Other Things That Fly

I heard the knock on the door about eight o'clock that night. Right around the time it was dawning on me how tired I was.

I figured it was Molly. Needing something. She had just brought Frank home an hour or two earlier, and I was on standby for any help she might need.

"Who is it?" I called through the door. Too tired and lazy to walk over and look through the peephole.

"It's me. Wilbur."

A brief silence. During which I realized I was disappointed. Which is weird, because Wilbur is one of my favorite people in the whole world. But I guess I'd been hoping it was Molly, wanting me to do something that involved seeing Frank.

I didn't say anything. So I guess Wilbur felt he had to.

"You didn't show up at school today. I wanted to make sure you were okay."

That made only partial sense. Because he also could have called.

I opened the door.

Wilbur stood in my hallway with an odd look on his face. Ruffled. Not literally. Just the look in his eyes. As if something had ruffled him. And the ruffled thing was also sort of an aura. A field of energy that I could have read with my eyes closed.

I could see and smell that he had been drinking.

Dangling from his left hand was a six-pack of beer.

"You okay?" I asked.

"Yeah. Fine."

I knew he wasn't, but I didn't feel the need to push it. Wilbur never pushed me to say anything.

"Come on in."

He did.

We stood in my living room, more awkwardly than usual.

"So how come you skipped school?"

"No special reason," I said. "Just tired. And in a funny mood."

So we both had information we weren't quite ready to let fly.

We sat out on the fire escape and drank all the beer. I had two and Wilbur had four.

We talked about school, ugly a topic as that is. We talked about Annabel and her new boyfriend. He told me Shane had dyed her hair green.

It was getting dark. It was getting late.

"I'm exhausted," I said. "I barely slept last night."

I thought that would be unsubtle enough for Wilbur. But he didn't move. Maybe he was too drunk to get the message. I watched the lights of cars moving along the street below us. Wondering if I should say more.

Then Wilbur said, "I was hoping I could stay here tonight."

"Oh. Yeah. Sure. Why didn't you just ask me?"

He never answered that one. We watched the cars for a few more minutes. It was a little too cool to be wearing only a T-shirt, which was actually a nice feeling. It was really going to act like autumn now. Finally.

"I had a fight with my stepfather," he said. "I can't go back there tonight."

"The couch is pretty comfortable."

"Sometimes I wish he would die." That just hung in the air for a moment. "I would never kill anybody. Or even hurt anybody. But I have these fantasies that he dies of some disease or something. Or gets hit by a car."

I winced at the reference. But I'm sure the darkness and the drunkenness covered it over.

"Then I have to go to confession," he said. "I think that's what I hate most about him. That he makes me hate. And I don't want to be a hater. I want to tolerate everybody. But he's just so in my face. It's like he challenges me to hate him."

"We should probably go to bed," I said. "Things will look better after some sleep."

"Did that upset you? What I just said?"

"No. I don't blame you. I'm just really tired."

I was lying in bed, in my room. With the lights out. But the door to the living room was open. In case Wilbur needed anything.

I heard his voice call in to me.

"Did you ever find out who it was that got hit?"

"Yeah. It was my friend Frank."

A brief silence. Then, "Holy shit."

"Yeah."

"Is he okay?"

"I think so. He's hurt pretty bad, though. I was at the hospital with him until this morning. That's why I was too tired to go to school."

I lay in that dark silence for a while. I thought he might have passed out or gone to sleep.

"So you're speaking to him again."

"Well. He's been kind of out of it. I was doing most of the speaking. But yeah."

"Do you still have a crush on him?"

My stomach tingled. I wanted to say, No, it's even more than a crush now. But of course I didn't.

"Yeah."

Long, long silence. Then I geared up to say something I never would have said to anyone but Wilbur. In fact, I wouldn't even have said it to Wilbur if the lights were on. If he were in the same room with me.

"What do you think that says about me?" A pause, but I filled it. "I've never had a serious boyfriend. Never really been in love. And then when I finally have all those feelings for somebody . . . Well, you know."

"Maybe it says you're looking for a man who's gentle. You know, more than most men are. I can relate. Because of my step-father. I'm looking for a man who's kinder than most men I meet. Maybe you are, too."

"That is such a good answer. I wish I'd asked you sooner."

We were quiet for a while, and I figured he wasn't going to say any more. So I said, "Good night."

Nothing. I had already lost Wilbur to sleep.

In the morning, he was gone. He'd left a note on the couch. Two words.

Thank you.

I guess there was nothing much more anybody needed to say.

It was five days later, and I was sitting in Frank's bedroom.

I'd waited five days for this chance. I had skipped school all week, just so I wouldn't miss any opportunity that came along. And now here I was.

Molly had gone out to shop for groceries and refill a prescription. And I was sitting here taking care of Frank. Well, sitting here. I'm not sure what I was supposed to do to take care of him. He just needed somebody around.

It wasn't exactly the way I'd dreamed it. After all that waiting, I had mixed feelings now. I guess I thought it would be like the hospital. Like I could look at him and touch his face and nobody would be any the wiser. Not literally. I knew he was awake. I was prepared to find him the way I did, sitting up in bed.

I just somehow pictured it being the way it was before.

I'm not sure why I still ever expect anything to be the way it was before.

"Toto is a lot better," I said. Just to have something to say. "He's all done with his pills."

I looked at Frank. He was looking back. Every time I looked

at him, his eyes bored right through mine. I felt like I had words printed inside my head and he was reading them with great interest.

After a pause, he said, "Toto was sick?"

I had no idea what to say to that.

He filled the gap for me.

"Sorry. I guess there's something there I should know, huh? Don't get too freaked out. I remember most things. Just a few days before the accident it gets spotty. It may all come back. Or some may. Hard to say. Anyway, it's just a few days."

"What about after? In the hospital?"

It came out before I really had time to think. There was no fetching it home again.

"I remember you were there," he said. "If that's what you mean."

I snuck a glance at him, but he was doing that thing again. Looking at the private inside of my head.

I was hoping he wouldn't say anything else. If he remembered more, I didn't want to hear about it. I didn't want to know.

I looked at his arm. Just to have someplace else to direct my eyes. He'd had orthopedic surgery on his arm, and it was in a sling, and wrapped loosely with what looked like an elastic bandage. It was bulky and huge. I'd heard there was an actual metal bar under those bandages. With pins that went right into the bones. But I'd been doing my best not to think about that.

He saw me looking.

"Hey," he said. Startling me. "Do me a favor, okay? Help me change the dressings on my arm. While Molly is gone. It has to be done every day. And Molly has been really nice about it, but she's so squeamish. I know she hates it. She'll be so happy if she gets home and it's already done. Let's surprise her."

I swallowed hard.

"What do you need me to do?"

"Come over here and sit on the bed."

I did as I was told. Sat beside his right arm.

"Now take my hand and support my arm while I unwrap this. It's a little bit heavier than you'll expect it to be, because of all that metal."

So I did what I was told again. I held Frank's hand. Supported his right arm. He was bandaged up to the base of his thumb. His hand felt rough. Calloused. A little small for a man's hand, I found myself thinking. But strong-looking. Short, wide fingers.

It gave me a great excuse not to look at his face.

"Is this going to hurt you?" I asked.

"Not if you keep my arm steady. I'm on so many painkillers I don't feel much. But if I have to use the muscles in that arm, the pain'll break right through the Vicodin, believe me. So don't let go."

"I won't."

He unwound the bandage until it fell away onto the bed. I sucked in a breath. Saw the metal bar, parallel to the bone in his arm. Two steel pins came down from it and disappeared between gauze patches. It made me a little queasy, even before he moved the gauze. After he pulled those pads away, I felt this sickening feeling like a sword moving down through my lower intestines. Something about those pins going right through his skin. I felt a little dizzy, like I might pass out.

No wonder Molly hated this so much.

His elbow stayed bandaged because the pins were all on the inside. Right inside the bones. Something else to try not to think about.

He handed me a tube of triple antibiotic ointment and a bunch of fresh gauze pads in little paper packages. They had been sitting on the bedside table, and he was able to reach them easily with his left hand.

"Now, set my arm down. Very carefully. And put a ton of that ointment in the middle of each pad. Okay? And then put two on each spot. One on each side of both pins."

"Sure," I said. If I don't pass out first, I didn't say.

He watched me work. I could feel it. I could barely see it in my peripheral vision. It made me nervous. I just kept looking down at his arm.

"Thank you for being there in the hospital with me," he said.

I never answered. I couldn't have talked if I'd tried.

"I would have been so scared waking up there all alone."

I placed a heavily ointmented gauze pad against one of the pins. I winced on Frank's behalf. But if it hurt, he didn't let on. Vicodin. Right. I wished I'd had some Vicodin myself right about then. Thirty, maybe.

"It shouldn't be that way," I said. Without knowing I was about to.

"What? I shouldn't be scared?"

"You shouldn't *have* to be. Why does it have to be a world where you can't even go to the hospital in peace? And please don't say, 'It just is that way.' I hate it when people say, 'It just is that way.' "

"I wasn't going to say that."

"Oh. Good." I placed another pad. Gingerly. "What were you going to say?"

"I'm not sure." A long pause. "The world doesn't always play by its own rules, Elle."

"Not entirely sure I follow."

He sighed. "I guess I mean we all pretty much agree on certain things. Equality and stuff like that. But whenever it turns up missing, people just let it slide. That's why there's such a thing as activism. Sometimes you have to jumpstart the world just to get it to be what even the world admits it should be."

I placed the last gauze pad with a sigh. Got up and dumped all the trash in the bathroom wastebasket. Then I came back and held Frank's hand again. Supported his arm while he wrapped it back up.

"I sort of like the idea of activism," I said. "Except that part of me doesn't. Yeah. Real articulate. I know. Let me think what I'm trying to say here. Sometimes I feel like people who want to oppress people . . . well, they need people to feel oppressed. Like it's a dance. Like it takes two, you know? And maybe they couldn't even do it without you. I'm still not saying it right. Sometimes I think fighting against something only makes it stronger."

I looked up briefly. Thank God he was not looking at me. He was still wrapping the bandage. Watching his own work.

He nodded slightly. "Sounds like what you're saying is that you have the luxury of opting out of prejudice. I don't."

"Yeah. Okay. Sorry if that was a stupid thing to say."

"Not at all. It was very intelligent. Very thoughtful. It's just a thought from *your* world. It's a little different over here. Not all activism is fighting against something, anyway. Sometimes it's more subtle. Just something you do to open people's eyes."

I'm not sure why, but I thought suddenly about the pictures I'd taken of Wilbur. I hadn't even bothered to develop them yet. They were still sitting in my camera.

"Do you think it's possible to be an activist using a camera?"

"It's more than possible. It's Molly's life's work."

At that moment, as if on cue, the front door opened and then slammed again.

Molly was back.

My private moment with Frank was over.

Thank God. And, also, damn.

The door to my apartment was standing wide open. My brain and body went cold. I thought I was being robbed. I thought maybe I should run, but I took one more step first, so I could halfway look inside.

I thought about my mother. But it couldn't be. She wouldn't dare. She promised. Even my mother wouldn't openly break a promise, just like that.

And yet, there she was. Standing at my kitchen table, shuffling through some papers. Some of *my* papers. Just homework. But it really pissed me off.

She hadn't seen me yet.

She picked up one of the papers to look at the text more closely. But she held it farther away from her face, not closer. As if she wished she had longer arms. I'm pretty sure she needed reading glasses and was refusing to admit it to anyone. Herself included.

I stepped inside. "You better not have let my cat out," I said. "He's just barely recovered. He still has stitches in his gums."

My mother looked up at me. "You've been skipping school."

"What happened to your promise about calling first? Not to mention knocking."

"That was before I found out you haven't bothered to go to school for days."

"Haven't *bothered* to? It's not like I'm just being lazy, Mother. There's been a lot going on around here."

"Tell me all about it."

"No thank you."

She said nothing. Just leveled me with a look that made me feel six years old and in trouble deep.

"I'll go back to school," I said. It wasn't such a big compromise. I'd already been planning to go back to school.

She just stood there, taking it all in. She was still holding my math homework, but she was holding it too tightly, and I wanted to tell her not to wrinkle it. But I didn't want us to be fighting. I was in a place where a mother might not have been a bad deal. Granted, my mother had always been more like a cheap mother substitute. But she was still the only one I had. And I didn't want to be fighting with her. So I didn't tell her to be careful how she held that paper.

Besides. I could always print out another copy.

As if she could read my mind, she set it back on the table. Then she walked over to my new couch and sat down.

"All right," she said. "I'm listening."

"Mark this day on your calendar," I said. Half under my breath. But she heard it.

I know she was hurt, but she spoke in soft, measured words. "I said I was listening. And I am."

I took a deep breath. There wasn't much of this I was prepared to say to my mother.

"My best friend has been in the hospital. He nearly died. He could have died."

"That young man next door?"

"Yes. Frank."

"I know why you like him so much. You think I don't but I do."

My gut went icy and a little sick. I said nothing.

"It's because he listens to you. Right? Right, Elle? He's your friend because he listens. I can hear subtext, you know."

I guess it was a strange thing to think, but I thought, Wow. She heard something. She really did.

"Talk to me," she said. "I'll listen. Tell me what's going on in your life."

I just stood there in front of her for what felt like a long time. I wasn't sure what I wanted to say.

"It's not quite that easy." Not after all these years.

She rose to leave.

"It's okay, Mother. Really. We're okay. All I'm saying is . . . baby steps."

She glanced at me over her shoulder on her way out the door.

"I'll go back to school now," I said.

"You bet your ass you will."

Then she was gone.

THIRTEEN

Mascara, and Other Things That Run

I wish I could say for a fact how much time passed by before the next really important thing happened. I'm thinking it was about ten or eleven days. Thing is, you don't know another big thing is about to happen. So you don't keep count. But it must've been around a week and a half.

I was sitting out on the fire escape. Even though it was getting really cool in the evenings now. I guess it must seem like I never did much of anything else but just sit out on my fire escape. But it's strangely addictive, watching the world move. I didn't have a TV. I didn't even really want one. And I liked the feeling of the seasons changing. I loved the feel of air that wasn't hot.

I looked down and saw a man walk out of the apartment house across the street. He was wearing an orange shirt and carrying a broom.

At first, I didn't think much about it at all. Other than maybe it was a little strange for somebody to sweep the street in front of his own apartment building. Unless he was the super or something.

Then after a few minutes, I started wondering why he looked familiar. He reminded me of somebody. I just couldn't for the life of me think who that might be.

When it hit me, it felt like it hit me almost literally. Like a fastball you take right in the gut. My whole body felt freezing cold, but especially my stomach.

I thought, No. It couldn't be. They couldn't have let him out. They were supposed to keep him locked up forever. For the rest of his life, so nobody could get hurt.

I had this flash of memory. Sitting on the fire escape with Frank for one of the first times ever. He said when Harry was back on his meds, he was the nicest, quietest neighbor you could possibly want.

I wondered what Frank would say about Harry now.

I crawled back in through the window and got my camera, and my big, long close-up lens. Before I ran to Molly and Frank with this, I wanted to be absolutely sure.

I crawled back out on the fire escape and watched him through the camera sight. It had one of those viewfinders that sights right through the lens.

It was him all right. My body got all cold again. I wanted to run tell them right away. But first I snapped off a couple of shots. There was something weirdly precise about all of his movements. Like he might miss a piece of dust if he swept too fast. I wasn't sure if I could get that on film. What it would look like with the action frozen. But I was in a period of discovery. Experimentation. I tried to get everything on film. Otherwise, how would I know?

Thing is, I hadn't been developing anything. Even the photos of Wilbur were still sitting in little film canisters, undeveloped. Like I'd been too tired and too busy and too much just barely coping with all this newness to follow through. Like I might not be strong enough to get the feedback on how I had done.

When I'd taken a few more photos I might never develop, I ran next door. Knocked on the door.

"Who is it?" I heard Molly call through the door.

"It's me. Elle. Molly, he's back. Crazy Harry. He's back."

The door opened. I looked at her face. Her eyes looked lost and far away. Hurt. Not really furious like I'd expected. And not really shocked.

"Okay," she said. "Thanks for telling me."

I just stood there. Waiting for something more, I guess. Something easier to recognize.

"Why'd they let him out?" I asked.

Like she would know.

"I guess if he's back on his meds, they probably judged him not a danger to himself. Or to others."

"Why didn't they put him in jail? Somebody could have died because of him." I heard myself speak as if I were standing outside myself. And I thought it sounded strange, the way I said "somebody." Like I couldn't bring myself to say who.

"He doesn't belong in jail, Elle. He has a mental illness."

"Well, he doesn't belong on our street, either."

"Well, he has to be somewhere."

Then the doorway was empty. She didn't close the door. Just stepped back from the doorway. Into her apartment. When she appeared again, she was wearing her big sun hat.

I wondered if Frank was asleep.

I followed her down the stairs and outside.

She crossed the street, but I didn't. I just watched. I still had my camera hanging from its strap around my neck. I couldn't hear what they were saying to each other. But I could see their body language. The way they leaned in toward each other. Like they were sharing some sort of confidence. I snapped off a couple dozen photos with my close-up lens.

When she came back across the street, I was wired and not sure what to say. I wanted to know what she'd said to him. But it didn't feel like any of my business. It felt like a private place. Someplace where I had no right to trespass.

But I think she must have seen the disbelief in my eyes.

"It's not like he ever meant Frank any harm," she said.

"So you forgive him."

"I know I wouldn't have said this when it first happened. I would've probably taken the guy apart with my bare hands. But, in a way, there's really nothing to forgive. It was just sort of a freak accident. I mean, all he did was make a sudden noise."

"So you forgive him."

"Yeah. I guess."

"Does Frank forgive him?"

"I don't know. I haven't asked him."

Then she went back inside.

I looked up to see Crazy Harry, still across the street. Leaning on his broom. Watching her go.

It was much later that evening. Dark. And the temperature was perfect. That perfect crisp autumn night.

Or so I thought.

I was sitting out on the fire escape. And I heard a little sound. A familiar sound, but I hadn't heard it for a while. It was the sound of Frank's window opening next door.

I watched, almost in disbelief, as he very carefully climbed out onto his own part of the fire escape. He was using only his left hand, and being extra slow and cautious. I think he knew I was there, but he hadn't actually looked at me yet.

When he'd settled himself with his back up against the building, he said, "Hey."

Just kind of quiet. Still not looking at me.

But it felt good, because it felt familiar.

"Hey," I said back.

Then we just sat for a while. Maybe five minutes. Or maybe less, and maybe it just felt like five minutes. I had this deep feeling that felt suspiciously like being happy. It was an actual physical feeling, around in my gut. Like something priceless had been returned to me. Just as I was accepting that I'd never see it again.

Then Frank said, "I have to tell you something."

The feeling left.

"Okay. Tell me."

Silence.

I looked away. Looked at the building across the street and one over. Through one of the windows I could see a couple fighting. Not hitting, just screaming at each other. Even though I couldn't hear the screaming. I watched them because watching them kept my eyes turned away.

"I hate to even tell you," he said.

"I caught that."

I could feel that sensation again. Like when I found Frank's glasses lying in the street. In the blood. That sense that my feelings just closed up shop and went home. All quiet on the western front.

"We have to move back to South Carolina. We can't afford to stay here."

He waited for a minute. Maybe to see if I wanted to talk. I didn't. I just watched that couple. The man kept walking away and the woman kept following after him. But they just kept going around in a circle.

"We have lots of medical bills because, up to a hundred thousand dollars, my insurance only covers eighty percent. And I won't be able to work for months because I won't be using my right hand. So we don't have next month's rent. So we'll be leaving at the end of the month."

In the silence that followed, I did the math. Not on the medical bills. On the time we had left. Eleven days.

"What are you going to do for rent in South Carolina?"

"Molly's brother and sister-in-law have a little apartment over their garage. Sort of like a big guest room."

I didn't say anything for a time. The couple pulled the shade and then turned off the lights. I wondered if that meant they were already planning to make up, which seemed just about unfathomable enough to make my head explode.

"Do they accept you?"

"Yes and no. They don't really know me. They knew Franny."

"Did they accept Molly and Franny?"

"Better than most of Molly's relatives, I guess."

I really hate to admit that I winced a little at the image of Franny. Just the tiniest bit. Another of those feelings that you think should go away but it doesn't entirely. I guess all feelings are like that. Information doesn't affect them as much as you think it should.

"Well, thanks for telling me."

I crawled back into my apartment, even though the night was perfect and I had planned to stay out there until I was too tired to keep my eyes open any longer.

Toto had been sleeping on the couch, but he booked it when he saw me come back in.

I stood in the middle of my own living room for a minute. Or more. Like I couldn't remember what comes next. No, worse than that. Like I couldn't possibly make up anything that could even potentially come next. No matter how hard I tried.

Then I stuck my head out the window again.

Frank was still there. Just sitting. Staring off into the dark.

"Are you ever coming back?"

"I hope so. But it's probably going to take a couple of years."

I took my head back.

I went to bed. But I wasn't sleepy. And I didn't go to sleep.

Sometime after eleven—maybe even closer to midnight—I heard a knock at my door.

I hadn't been asleep.

"Who is that at this hour?" I yelled, without even getting up.

The voice came back a little muffled, but I managed to make out the words. "It's me. Wilbur."

I got up. Threw on a robe over the thousand-year-old FRANKIE SAY RELAX T-shirt I'd stolen from my mother to use as a sleep shirt. Answered the door.

I half expected him to look like he'd been beaten up or something. But if his stepfather had laid a hand on him, I couldn't see where. I could tell he'd been crying, though. His mascara streaked all the way down onto his cheeks. Startlingly black.

I looked down at his hands but they were empty.

"No beer," I said.

"I'm trying to cut down."

I snorted one single blast of something like laughter.

"You better come in," I said.

It was about two in the morning and I still couldn't sleep.

"Wilbur?" I said. Loud enough to sound like a whisper by the time it reached the living room. Or so I hoped.

"Yeah?"

"Are you asleep?"

"Obviously not."

"*Were* you asleep? Did I wake you?"

"No."

"Oh. Good."

Then I wasn't sure what to say.

"So . . . what?" he asked.

"I don't know. I'm not sure. I guess I just felt like talking."

No response. Then I looked up to see him standing in my bedroom doorway, wrapped in the blanket I'd given him. I wanted to see if he'd cleaned off all that mascara, but the only light came from behind him. The streetlight mostly shone through the living-room window. So I couldn't see his face.

I moved over a little and patted the bed beside me, and he came and lay down. Huddled tightly in the blanket. As if it were about twenty degrees in there.

"How's Frank?" he asked. Quietly.

"Better."

"Good."

"He's moving away."

"Oh. Bad."

"Yeah. Very bad."

"When did you find out?"

"Just earlier tonight."

"Are you okay?"

"I don't think so. But I can't really tell yet. I know that sounds retarded."

"No. It doesn't. I never feel things until later."

"Really?"

"Yeah. Really."

Silence. Silence. Silence. I wanted to say more about Frank leaving. So many more things. Only . . . what were they?

"I keep wanting to tell him I'm sorry for the way I treated him. You know. After I found out."

"So why don't you?"

"Because I think he might not remember it. I know he doesn't remember a lot from those last few days before the accident. He didn't even remember that Toto was sick. So I'm thinking maybe he doesn't even know what a jerk I was. Don't get me wrong. It's not that I'm trying to weasel out of it. It's more that . . . Well, if he doesn't know I did something to hurt him, then he isn't hurt. Right? So if I tell him . . . Only, what if he does remember?"

The mental twisting and turning was making my brain hurt, so I stopped to rest. For quite a few beats.

Wilbur didn't say anything.

"What would *you* do? If it were you?"

A pause while he thought that over.

"I think I'd go with the living amends."

"The what?"

"Living amends. That's when you just don't do the thing you're sorry for anymore. You just do better. Some people think that's better than words anyway."

"Both might be best."

"Yeah, but it's like you said. If he doesn't know, then he's not hurt. You might be opening a can of worms."

I gave all that a minute to soak in. Find a place to sit down.

Then I said, "I met Frank the very first day I moved in here. My mother was just throwing me out, and I'd never lived alone before. And I was scared to live alone. But I never really did live alone because he was there. Right from the start, he was there. So I was never really alone. But if some strangers move in next door . . ." The thought was so horrible that it stopped me in midsentence. I hadn't tried on that image before. Strangers in Frank and Molly's apartment.

Wilbur spoke up before I could get back on track.

"I know it's not really much," he said. "But you do have me. And Shane and The Bobs."

Did I have Shane and The Bobs? After the way I'd been treating them? But I figured Wilbur must know, so I said, "That's true."

"Probably not much consolation."

"Some," I said.

Then we didn't talk for a long time, and I wasn't sure if we would ever start up again. I figured I might just lie awake all night looking at the outlines of him in the dark.

Next thing I knew, I opened my eyes and it was light. My eyes felt grainy and sore, and my stomach was a little rocky. Almost like a hangover.

Wilbur lay fast asleep beside me, still mummified in his blanket. The streaks of mascara still marking his face. Still betraying the fact that he really did feel. Whether delayed or not didn't seem to matter much in the light of dawn.

FOURTEEN

Mocha Almond Fudge and Loss.
The Perfect Companions.

After Wilbur left, I spent most of that next day dancing.

Sounds happier than it actually is.

I have this thing about Janis Joplin. Her music, that is. Not Janis herself, who, of course, is long dead.

I think I want to be her.

Only not dead.

Anyway. It's the music. People might expect I'd be put off by the fact that it was all recorded a quarter of a century before I was born. They would be wrong.

I have a bunch of it on an iPod. A different one than I have all my mixed music on. So after Wilbur left, I stuck the earbuds in and just got into it. And none of that "Me and Bobby McGee" crap, either. We don't need no stinking slow ballads. Thirty-two really hard-rock tracks, and every other one was "Piece of My Heart." I just can't get enough of that one. Never really could.

I still had one beer in the fridge, left over from the weird, upsetting party. I drank it all during the first play of "Piece of My Heart," and then used the bottle as a microphone. It's sort of like playing air guitar, only with singing. I didn't actually sing. Just mouthed the words perfectly into the beer bottle and moved my body, and every time I opened my mouth, this perfect Janis Joplin shriek coincided.

It's very satisfying in a way I can't really explain. Believe me, I've tried. It also makes me tired, which I appreciate when I'm feeling crappy.

I think I'd been at this for somewhere between two and three hours when I saw my front door open. I pulled out the earbuds.

In walked my mother.

Before I could even open my mouth, she said, "Now, don't say I should have called, because I've been calling you for hours."

"I had music on."

"But you can't say I didn't try."

"Why did you come over if I didn't answer the phone? Didn't you figure I was out?"

"I took a chance," she said. "I needed to talk to you. It's important."

Only then did it hit me. Things were not okay with her.

I honestly thought, at least from the look on her face, that she was having a worse day than I was. If such a thing was possible.

She sat at my kitchen table with her forehead in one palm. I'd made her a cup of tea, and it sat on the table right under her face, and the steam swirled up like she was getting a facial, or trying to breathe steam to clear her sinuses. Actually, she did look like she'd been doing some crying.

She still wasn't telling me what this was all about.

"What's up, Mother?"

She took a sip of the hot tea. Made a face. "Don't you have any coffee?"

"No. Sorry. I don't drink coffee."

"But I got you that nice coffeemaker."

"That had a little accident."

"Oh." Long silence. Long, awkward. Heavy. Strange. "Donald broke up with me."

"Oh. Sorry." I guess that was at least half true. I wasn't sorry Donald was gone. I couldn't be. But I was sorry he'd made her feel like this. Guys like that always will, I think. Not that I'm this big expert on guys or anything. But it seemed obvious to me. Like, whatever he is now. Whatever it is right now, that's what it's always going to be.

"I thought this might be a good moment to discuss the best time for you to move."

"Move?"

"Come home."

She was still staring down at the table, forehead in her palm.

I couldn't answer. I just couldn't force out any words. I could feel that my mouth was too wide open, so I focused on closing it again.

After a while, she looked up.

"Well?"

"Mother. I'm not coming home."

Looking back, it seems I might at least have considered it.

What with Frank moving away. And me being a little scared about living alone. But I didn't consider it. Not for a second. It was impossible. I knew that the minute it hit my ears. Some things, like independence, only go one direction. Independence has no reverse gear. Fear or no fear.

"What do you mean? Of course you're coming home. I'm so sorry I put you through this, darling. I lost my head. But it's over now. We can go back to the way things were before."

"No. We can't, Mother. We can't go back to the way things were before. It's impossible."

She looked into my eyes for a minute, then started to cry. I guessed that meant she saw.

"You know," she said, "I pay your rent. You can only live here as long as I pay your rent. I could insist you come home."

I wanted to be mad, but I just felt too sorry for her. I didn't even feel like I needed to fight her now. Fighting is for when you're not sure if you're strong enough to win. When you have to test it out. When you know who's stronger, you don't have to fight. You can be invited to a fight and just choose not to show.

"I know you wouldn't do that," I said.

She fell all into sobbing, her head down on her arms on my table.

I came around behind her, and put my arms around her, and just let her cry it out.

After she left, I couldn't get the Janis thing going again. It's like she stole all my wind.

So I sat on the fire escape for an hour or so, wishing Frank would come out and sit with me. But he never did. Then I re-membered that Molly was taking him to an appointment with the orthopedic surgeon. Something about getting an X-ray of the pins in his elbow to check them for something.

I think it was around two or three in the afternoon when I heard a knock at the door.

I climbed back inside to go see who it was.

Freaking Grand Central Station, I was thinking. I was wishing that at a time like this everybody would just leave me alone.

I opened the door to see Wilbur, Shane, and The Bobs standing in my hall. Big Bob was carrying a paper grocery sack.

Shane's hair was indeed green. Quite noticeably green.

So, I guess I did have Shane and The Bobs. I guess Wilbur had been right.

I said, "I hope that grocery sack is full of beer. I could use some."

Shane said, "Wilbur's trying to cut down."

I nodded. As if I'd known that. But, truthfully, I'd really thought that was only a joke.

"Can we come in?" Also Shane. "We come bearing ice cream."

"Ice cream?" I wasn't quite getting it yet.

Wilbur said, "I hope you don't mind. I told them you were feeling bad. You know. About Frank moving away."

For a minute, I was stunned. I felt like that was so out of character for Wilbur. He doesn't just run off and tell people what you told him. But then I put two and two together with the ice cream. And it hit me. Wilbur knew I needed help. So he brought me some.

So, maybe that's why I had Shane and The Bobs. Because of Wilbur. Because he told them . . . what? That I needed them? That I wasn't as bad as they thought? I had no idea.

162

I only know that I was suddenly able to see, as if through someone else's eyes, that I needed help. Much more so than I'd realized.

Trouble was, I still mostly wanted to be left alone. I've practiced "alone" a lot, and I'm good at it.

I'm guessing this must all have shown on my face. Because they began inventorying the ice cream. Big Bob set the bag down on the hall carpet, and Little Bobby took the quart cartons out one by one, held them up in a perfect impression of Vanna White, and announced their flavors.

"Chocolate chip mint . . ."

A few soft oohs and aahs from Shane.

"Rocky road . . ." He scrambled into the bag for another. "Mocha almond fudge . . . butter rum . . . and last but not least . . . chocolate chip cookie dough!"

A few more oohs and aahs.

"That would be a shitload of ice cream," I said.

"Nothing's too good for our friend," Little Bobby said.

I just stood there for the longest time. Not knowing what to say. I don't do grief in a crowd.

Finally, I said the only thing I could think to say. "Mocha almond fudge, huh?"

Little Bobby said, "A whole quart all for you, if that's your favorite."

"I guess you'd better come in."

We sat in a circle on my living-room hardwood. Cross-legged, like some kind of campfire circle or Native American sweat lodge. Except we each had a spoon.

163

Four of the cartons of ice cream sat in the middle of the circle, looking a bit liquidy around their peripheries. The mocha-almond-fudge carton sat in the middle of my crossed legs, nearly one-third polished off. The sugar rush was making me feel emotionally numb. I liked the feeling.

"Okay," Shane said. "Enough small talk. Who wants to be the first to tell their very worst breakup story?"

"Ooh," Little Bobby said. "That's hard. I have so many to choose from."

"Breakup story," I repeated.

"Yeah." Shane.

"I'm not breaking up with anybody. I was never with him in the first place."

"So? It's still a loss."

"But it's not a breakup."

"Okay," Shane said. "Who wants to be the first to share the worst, most painful loss they ever had that wasn't actually a breakup?"

Three hands shot up. Shane, answering her own question, and both Bobs.

I ate another big spoon of ice cream. I hadn't asked for this. Wouldn't have asked for it. But some weird part of me wanted to hear the stories. Don't ask me why, but the idea of hearing about other people's heartache sounded strangely appealing.

I looked over at Wilbur, and he looked a little green around the gills.

"You okay, Wilbur?"

"I don't think I want to play this game," he said. "It sounds painful."

"You don't have to go if you don't want."

He didn't answer. He just kept looking down into the mint-chocolate-chip carton.

"I'll go," Little Bobby said. "It was my pediatrician. I was madly in love with my pediatrician. Until I was fourteen. Which, on the one hand, was really humiliating, when your parents still send you to a pediatrician at fourteen. But on the other hand, I sure as hell wasn't about to argue for a new doctor. Anyway, I was sick a *lot*."

A smattering of laughter. No, not even laughter, really. Just little snorts of sound.

"And then one day he got me on the table and really read me the riot act. He said I wasn't sick and I was wasting his time and wasting my parents' money and I should go home and act like a healthy boy and stop all this nonsense. I was so incredibly humiliated. I slunk out of there feeling about an inch high, and then when I was passing by the desk, his two receptionist-type women were laughing behind their hands about something, and I was sure they were laughing at me. Now I think maybe they were just telling a joke or something. But at the time, it hit me all at once that if the doctor knew, then maybe everybody knew. I felt like the whole world was laughing at my most important secret. I went home and went to bed and didn't get up for six days."

Silence. I shoveled in more ice cream. I had no idea what you say about a thing like that.

Shane said, "Done?"

Bobby nodded once.

"There was this girl when I was thirteen. She was in my history class. We used to write all these notes in class. And they got more and more . . . well, you know. It's kind of personal. Anyway, we were making plans. You know. In the notes. Like a romantic thing. But then she got cold feet. And she not only didn't want to be my girlfriend, she didn't even want to talk to me. Or look at me. Except one day she cornered me in the girls' room and said she wanted to borrow the notes back. She knew I saved every one. She said she wanted to see what they said. Like, how incriminating they'd be. So I loaned them to her, even though they were just about the most important thing I owned. And she took them home and burned them. I know it sounds stupid. It was just a stack of papers. But it was the closest I'd ever come to having a girlfriend. I was so brokenhearted I stayed home from school for a week. I came to dinner every night with sunglasses on."

I couldn't help interjecting here. "What did your parents say?"

"Nothing. They didn't notice."

"How can you not notice sunglasses at the dinner table?"

"Well, they didn't let on that they noticed. I tried to get them to let me transfer to another school, but I wouldn't say why, and it didn't fly. So I wore my sunglasses in school for the rest of the year, and stayed as far away from the note burner as I could. Are we depressing you?"

"Sort of. But I was sort of depressed to start with. So it's okay."

After a bit of an awkward pause, Big Bob said, "You have to promise not to think I'm totally sick if I tell you I was in love with my cousin."

He paused for reaction, but no one reacted. Just a lot of spoon action.

"Actually, he was just a second cousin. It's not like I thought we'd get married or anything. It's just that he was really handsome, and a couple years older, and he was smart and athletic and funny and he was nice to me. So I admired him, you know?

Looked up to him. I loved him, but in a lot of ways. Anyway, when I was thirteen, we were at this family party for another cousin's wedding. And he took me out and got me high. So we were hanging out in the bushes in the dark, smoking weed and talking. And I thought I could really trust him. So I told him I was gay. He didn't say much. Just listened. But then the next day I found out he told everybody. *Everybody.* My parents. All of our relatives. All his friends from school. And I never really saw him again. I mean, if you don't count from across a room."

I looked down into my ice cream carton and was stunned to see I was an inch or two from the bottom of the quart.

"That's so sad," I said.

Big Bob said, "Which one of them?"

"All of them."

Shane said, "Should we have just kept shut?"

"No. No. I'm actually glad you told me. It actually almost sort of helps in a weird way. Not that it changes anything, really. But it's like you get this thing in your head where you think life's being unfair to you. And from the outside it looks like it's being more fair to everybody else. But then you hear more about the inside of them, and you feel like . . . I don't know. I don't know how to say it. Like it's just life. Like life is unfair to everybody sooner or later, and it just happens to be my turn. You know?"

Only, really, if I was to be completely honest, life was being fairer to me than most. Because Frank hadn't hurt or betrayed or humiliated me. He just had to go.

Silence. I dipped again with my spoon and hit the bottom of the carton. My knees and hip joints and sitting bones were aching from sitting cross-legged so long. But I didn't move.

Wilbur spoke up suddenly. "I'm going next, then."

I said, "You don't have to, Wilbur."

"No. I'm going. If it helps you, then I'm going."

I scraped the bottom of my ice cream carton while he gathered himself up to go.

"When I was eleven, my mother had this boyfriend named Enrique. And Enrique had this brother. Esteban. And Esteban came and lived with us for a while. And he paid a lot of attention to me. A lot. He played games with me. We went for walks. He taught me how to fish. He cooked special lunches for me. Refried beans and tortillas from scratch. We even sat on the couch every night and watched TV together, just the two of us. I'd never gotten much attention before. So I thought the sun rose and set on him. And then one time, after about five months, my mom and Enrique went away for the weekend and left me alone with Esteban. And he molested me. And not in that sort of statutory-but-not-really-forcible way, either. He was rough. And I was scared. And he hurt me a lot. And then, I don't know if he felt guilty, or if he was just afraid he'd get in trouble, but he took off and I never saw him again. And I missed him so much. I know that sounds weird. But I missed him every minute of every day. I hated what he did. I didn't want him to come back and do it again. I wanted him to come back and be nice to me like before. But . . . this is the really weird part . . . I've never said this to anybody, so the next part stays right here in this room, okay?"

He looked to each of us in turn, collecting four solemn nods. Shane even put her hand over her heart.

"I didn't want him to come back and hurt me, but if I'd only had two choices, I would have chosen having him molesting me over not having him at all." Silence. "Is that really sick?"

"It's really sad," I said.

"No," Shane said. "It's just human. Kids need attention. They'll pay anything."

Nobody said anything for a long time. I just scraped the last of my mocha almond fudge out of the carton and thought about something I'd never considered before. I thought about how little attention anybody had really paid me. At least, until I met Frank.

Later that night, right after they left, I stuck my head out the window. Frank was out on the fire escape. Just staring off into the dark. So I quick climbed out.

"Hey," he said.

"Hey."

"I was hoping you'd come out."

"Oh. My friends were here."

"So, you're still friends with them. That's good. I guess you got around whatever you were mad at them for?"

"It wasn't their fault, anyway. It was my fault."

"Well, anyway. I'm glad you came out. I thought maybe you didn't want to talk to me."

I didn't answer at first, because I didn't know what to say. Then I said, without knowing I was about to, "Do I owe you an apology?" Something about Frank thinking I wasn't speaking to him, I guess.

"No," he said. Very fast and definite. "Do I owe you one?"

"No. Why would you owe me an apology?"

"Maybe I should have told you sooner. Like when we first started being friends."

So he did remember.

The sudden change of direction made my stomach turn. I guess the quart of mocha almond fudge wasn't helping. I wanted to ask if we could talk about something else. But I couldn't say that to Frank.

So I just said, "You didn't do anything wrong."

And we sat for a while without talking.

While we were doing that, I decided that not talking is like a litmus test for a real friend. You can just sit there and be. Not always be filling up the air with words.

After a while, I figured I'd have to go in soon. I had to go to the bathroom, and I hadn't fed the cat. I said something unusually honest.

I said, "I have no idea what to do with how much I'm going to miss you."

He digested that for a minute. Didn't leap up to try to fix it like most people would.

"You know," he said, "there are a variety of communication devices than can bridge the gap between New York and South Carolina."

"What will they think of next?" I said, playacting as if I hadn't known. "Are you going to have e-mail?"

"Even if I have to do dial-up. But hopefully we'll be able to afford high-speed. You could e-mail me and tell me about your day."

"That would be nice. Would you e-mail me back?"

"Of course I would. The longest e-mails I can bring myself to type with my left hand."

We sat quiet for a minute more, and then I said I had to go in.

"I wish I didn't have to leave, too," he said.

"I'm scared that people will be more prejudiced in South Carolina. I'm worried about you."

"I survived it the first time."

"Well," I said. "Good night, I guess."

"Good night, Elle."

For some weird reason, it felt good to hear him say my name. I knew it wouldn't be the same to see it in an e-mail typed with his left hand.

Then, on the other hand, I'm guessing that Shane's note burner and Little Bobby's pediatrician and Big Bob's second cousin and Wilbur's mother's boyfriend's brother hadn't encouraged them to keep in touch by e-mail.

Maybe I should just have been happy for what I got.

FIFTEEN

Say Something Brilliant Before You Go

The last time I got to spend any serious time with Molly was the day she let me use her darkroom. Of course, I didn't know enough to use it on my own. She helped me. Together we developed the Wilbur pictures.

Well. Mostly she developed them. But I was there.

We didn't say much at first. I think I was a little nervous about how they'd turn out.

When Molly hung up the first few prints to dry, I could barely contain my disappointment. Whatever I'd seen in my head I hadn't caught on film. They were just ordinary snapshots. At best.

I withdrew. I went and sat with my back against the wall. Out of the corner of my eye, I watched her work in the dim red glow. I was feeling like I'd miss her when she moved away, but I didn't know how to say it.

I was wondering what I'd say to Wilbur when he asked how his photos turned out.

After a few discouraging minutes, I heard her say, "Wow."

I quick got over there to see what she saw.

Among dozens more losers, she had just hung up what I could only describe as the perfect Wilbur photo.

It's hard to describe what makes a perfect photo of someone. The best I can say is that I think I photographed more than was actually there.

No, that's not saying it right. Because my camera didn't add anything to Wilbur.

It's like I saw something more through the lens. Something I swear I couldn't have seen with just my eyes. At least, I had never seen it before, and I was getting to know Wilbur pretty well. It was as though I had photographed right through his eyes into everything that had ever hurt him. It was all written there, like notes on a wall, and yet his overall look was not wounded. He was calm, steady. Almost proud. He was more than I'd ever seen Wilbur be. I guess he was himself.

And I had just caught the whole thing right there. And I had frozen it forever. Like proof.

"This is amazing," Molly said, and I felt that same sense of spreading warmth that I felt the other time she praised me.

I felt the need to push it away again.

"But the rest of these are such crap."

"We're not done yet. Besides. You got one really great one."

"But I took, like, seventy photos."

"Right. That's what photographers do. We take seventy photos to get one that's really worth keeping."

"We do?"

"We do if we're lucky. If we're good. If not, the numbers are even bigger."

"You know, Molly," I said. And then paused. "I'm going to miss *you*, too." I didn't say, Until a minute ago, I thought I'd only miss Frank. I didn't need to. It was painfully clear.

She surprised me with a big side hug, her arm around my shoulder, pulling me in closer to all that plump warmth.

"You're a sweet girl," she said.

"I wasn't always sweet."

"I wasn't exactly perfect, either."

So I guess we still were both holding on to our own personal trespasses.

I said, "You know I was never judging Frank for what he is, right?"

"Yeah," she said. "I know." A long silence. It felt a little tense. But maybe it's harder to know what to make of something in the mostly dark. No, I take it back. It's easier. "I know you were confused. Because you had a crush on Frank." I noticed she used the past tense. Like it was all done and gone now. "But you see . . . that's the other reason I was mad."

"Oh," I said. That made so much sense I wondered why I hadn't thought of it on my own. I didn't exactly say I was sorry. What's the point of being sorry for what you feel? "It's not like I did it on purpose," I said.

"Right. I know."

Maybe this is not healthy, but I think I slightly enjoyed the feeling that she took me seriously enough to even barely think of me as a threat.

I noticed she hadn't said she would miss me, too. But we can only ask for just so much.

We finished developing and hanging the photos, and there

was not even one more really good one. But I wasn't sure that mattered. I would take the one perfect one, and hand it to Wilbur. And I knew he would say, Wow. I knew he wouldn't say, But what about the others?

On the day they were actually leaving, I sat out on the stoop in front of our apartment house and read a book. Rather than my usual position on the fire escape.

I wanted to be able to say goodbye one more time.

I'd gotten caught up in an exciting part of the book, and I didn't even realize Molly was standing over me until I heard her voice.

"I guess this is it," she said.

I put down my book and looked up at her. Shading my eyes from the sun with one hand. "Yeah. I guess."

She was wearing her big sun hat, and she had a tote bag slung over her shoulder that looked like it must weigh about 142 pounds. She set down a soft-sided pet carrier she'd been holding. Either Gracie or George.

"I'll miss you," she said.

That pretty much turned all my thinking upside down.

"You will?"

"Yeah. I will. Don't sound so amazed."

"Why? What have I done that I deserve to be missed?"

"Well. You took an interest in photography. No, more than that. You took an interest in the world. Through your camera lens. And you're good at it. And you were a good friend."

"Better late than never," I said.

Silence while I tried it all on. Waited to see if it would fit.

Before that moment, I had accepted the status of only aspiring to what I admired. Now, if I was to believe Molly, I had to move myself up a rung.

Thing is, I always believed Molly.

I looked up to see Frank standing at the top of the stairs. Holding the other cat carrier in his left hand. His shattered right arm was supported in a sling. He didn't bandage his head anymore, and his hair was partly grown back in. Nearly halfway to the buzz cut he'd had when I met him.

He started down the stairs.

I swallowed. Didn't even try to speak.

Molly stepped into the street and raised one hand for a cab. There's never a cab when you need one, right? Wrong. A cab pulled up in front of her, as if the driver had been twenty feet away and just waiting for a signal.

So I guess we didn't have much time.

Frank stopped right in front of me. Set the carrier on the bricks by his feet.

I could see, through his short hair, where the stitches had been. It was still discolored and a little out of shape. But it was better than looking him right in the eye.

"So," he said.

"So."

Silence. I wondered if the meter was running.

"I'm not sure what to say," Frank said.

"Okay. Let me give you your cue. This is where you say something really monumental to me. Some quote I can write on my mirror. You know. To guide my life now that you're gone."

Truthfully, I'm not sure what I was going on about. Just filling dead air, I guess.

Frank raised one eyebrow. "Who says?"

"Well, if this were a movie, it would be time for your big line."

"It's not a movie, though."

"I still think you should say something profound."

"Gee, thanks. But no pressure, right?"

I laughed. Nobody moved. The cabdriver did not honk.

"Okay, how about this?" he said. An uncomfortable pause. At least, uncomfortable for me. "Always be the idiot who says 'I love you' and then starts to cry. Because that other idiot, she's not even worth being. You'd only be wasting your time trying to be her."

I squeezed my eyes closed, and when I opened them again, he was still there. I thought about hugging him, but I didn't. I was scared. Scared of what? It's a long list. Take your pick. Hurting his poor right arm. How his body would feel. How it would feel to me to get that close. How Molly would feel watching. I could go on.

"Well . . . ," he said. And started to move away.

I squeezed my eyes closed again. Knowing I'd had a chance to say goodbye properly and I let it go by. It would be years before I got a do-over.

When I opened my eyes again, Frank was right there. Standing in front of me. He'd come back.

He kissed me on the forehead and walked away.

While he was getting in the cab, I felt the kiss still there on my forehead. Literally. It was frozen there. I could still feel it. I wanted to bronze it, like people do with baby shoes. I wanted to mount it and hang it over my mantelpiece. If I'd had one.

But I knew it would be gone right around the same time Frank was.

He waved once, left-handed, from the back window as they drove away.

I sat out on the fire escape for most of the rest of the day.

I watched the cabs bunch up and slow down and then move again. Listened to the sirens. All those personal disasters happening somewhere, to someone. Smelled smoke drift up from the street, and watched the light change as the afternoon set in. I was noticing how this was home now. How much this felt like home.

After a while, I noticed Harry across the street, sweeping the sidewalk with a broom. I didn't know if he did that as part of his rent, or if it was because he got extra clean when he was on his meds. Just like he got extra dirty when he was off them. He was still being kind of strangely careful, like some tiny little piece of dirt might get by him. I watched him work for a time, and I don't think he ever knew I was up there watching.

Then I looked down again a minute later and saw that Harry had laid down his broom, and he was standing in the street, looking down. There wasn't much traffic, and what there was just kind of spilled around him. I watched him for a minute, wondering what was so fascinating. What he thought he saw.

Then it hit me, like a baseball bat to my gut, that he was looking at the exact spot in the street where Frank got hit.

I climbed in through the window and got my camera and ran downstairs two steps at a time.

I thought Harry would be gone, but he wasn't. He was still standing in the street, staring down at that spot.

I took a couple of photos, and then he looked up at me. Looked right into my camera lens, the way you would look into somebody's eyes.

His eyes looked deep and sad, like he'd just seen into a world of hurt that most of us will never know. And I'm not sure it was even all about Frank's accident. Every time I saw Harry, he looked like that. Like he'd seen hell and come back to tell everybody about it, but he just couldn't bring himself to open his mouth yet.

I took a shot of that pain.

Then I lowered the camera.

"Is that okay?" I asked. "Is it okay to take pictures of you?"

"Maybe," he said. "Why do you take pictures?"

I realized that I had never talked to Harry before. I felt like I knew him. I'd even gotten to care about him in a strange sort of way. I'd been furious at him. Wanted to drive him out of the neighborhood. And then I guess I'd forgiven him. Kind of quietly, when I wasn't even looking. But I'd barely even stood at his level. I'd never looked right into his face. I'd mostly looked down at him from above.

Now we looked straight into each other's eyes.

A cab came by and swerved around Harry, the driver blaring on his horn.

"Come here," I said, and gently took Harry by his elbow. "You better get out of the street."

"Why do you take pictures?" he asked again.

We stood there on the sidewalk together in the fading light.

"I'm a photographer," I said. "It's what I do."

"But why?"

I thought that out, and breathed. "I'm trying to jumpstart the world."

"What does that mean?"

"I'm trying to remind the world to be what it knows it should be."

"Oh," he said. "Okay. Why do you take pictures of me?"

"Because . . . I want people to know you. I want them to know you're real."

"Ah." We stood there for another minute. Harry's head was down, hanging down a bit as if he felt cowed. "It was my fault," he said. "What happened to Frank. He never would have had to leave if it wasn't for me."

"You didn't do it on purpose. Why were you standing there looking at that spot?"

"Saying goodbye."

Then he turned and walked back across the street, and picked up his broom, and went back inside his building.

I stood there watching him go for just a minute. Then I looked both ways, and when there were no cars coming, I stepped into the street. I looked down at the spot.

It was just pavement. Just regular asphalt, like the asphalt all around it. Like the asphalt on any other street. No sign that anything important had happened here. It was all cleaned and normal, and everything that happened that day could just have been a bad dream. But it wasn't. It wasn't a dream.

I looked in the direction Frank's cab had gone.

"Goodbye, Frank," I said.

Then I went back inside.

About an hour later, I was sitting on the couch. Next thing I knew, Toto jumped up onto my lap. I reached out to touch him but he jumped away again, onto the couch. But I held my hand out, and he came up and rubbed underneath it with his head.

I scratched him behind the ears and he purred. Then I scooped him up and pulled him onto my lap again. His body went tight, but then he stuck his head under my arm, where it was dark. I stroked his back, and felt him start to loosen up. After a while, he started to purr again, and the way I was holding him up against me, I felt the purring right against my heart.

I was hugging my cat.

We sat that way for a long time. Maybe an hour. It meant more to me than if I'd gotten a friendly cat. If a friendly cat had done this with me, that wouldn't have been such a big thing. But this was Toto.

"Poor Toto," I said. "See? That's not so hard. You just have to take a deep breath and let somebody love you."

Then I decided to call my mother. Just in case she was lonely or feeling down, and needed to talk.

SIXTEEN

So, After About Two Months of Small Talk

From: mollynfrank
To: independence16
3:22 p.m.

Dear E,
Hope you're having fun slogging through
the big snow. Saw it on the news. That's
one thing I don't miss. The seasonal
difference here is more subtle. About 20
degrees cooler and fewer palmetto bugs.
You don't want to know more about
palmetto bugs, believe me. We have
spiders here the size of your palm. No
kidding. And the cooler it gets, the more
they're found indoors. M found one in the
tub this morning. Nearly had a seizure.

I had to put him out more or less one-handed. We had one glass in the whole house big enough to catch him in.

But good news, too. I got a job. Well, just a part-timer from home. I've gotten so good at typing with my left that I got some casual work inputting data. They pay by the page, not the hour. So they have no investment in how many hands I use. This improves the outlook for getting back to the city. M and I crunched some numbers today, and if things keep going just like this, we might be able to pull it off in 14 or 15 months.

Won't miss the palmetto bugs.
What about you? Hope you're not feeling too alone.
-F

From: independence16
To: mollynfrank
6:16 p.m.

F,
Alone? What's that?
Hard to feel alone when Wilbur is here about three nights out of five. He even has his own roll-away bed stashed in my

living-room closet now. But it's not a
complaint. I like having him here. He's
good company. And it does sort of take
the alone out of living alone.

Christmas break is almost over. School
starts again in six days. Yeah, yeah, I
know. Just yesterday I told you school
starts again in seven days. Both true,
however. If I can survive school, you
can survive the palmetto bugs.

More later,
E

From: independence16
To: mollynfrank
11:11 p.m.

F,
Been wanting to say this but putting it
off. Wrestled with it last time I wrote
but lost. Tired of wrestling.

I didn't tell you this at the time, but
right after I found out you were
leaving, my friends came over and told
me all these horror stories about people
they'd lost. To make me feel better, I

guess. It did, in a way. But I didn't
want to feel better at their expense.
Didn't just want it to be "Somebody else
has it worse." But it sort of was. At
the time.

I've been thinking a lot since then.
Probably my first mistake.

I've been thinking how every one of
their stories was about giving all this
love to somebody who didn't even deserve
it. Somebody who turned on them or let
them down in some horrible way.

So then I started feeling lucky. Because
I made such a good choice. Even if
you're in some other part of the
country. Even if all we can ever be is
friends. At least you're somebody who
deserves it.

I guess I did one smart thing. To
balance off everything else.

Speaking of everything else, look at the
length of this e-mail. Geez.

I suppose you know I'm wrestling with
hitting delete. But I'm not going to.

I'm going to hit send. But first some
instructions for you: DO NOT SAY
ANYTHING.

DO NOT write back and say that's so
sweet and I'm a worthwhile person too or
any similar shit that will make me so
embarrassed my ears will turn red and
let off steam. Just read this and then
pretend you never did. It's just
information. Not an invitation to
comment.
E

PS: Did I mention that you should NOT
SAY ANYTHING?

From: mollynfrank
To: independence16
12:23 a.m.

Dear Elle,
My lips are sealed.
Love,
Frank